PRAISE FOR THE NOVELS BY ERIN QUINN

"Quinn's Beyond series features a near-perfect blend of lush romance and steamy passion with a wonderfully creative paranormal world. [Reader's experience an] instantly engaging, heart-wrenching and ultimately life changing relationship...life, love, sensation and emotion through a heroine to whom everything is new and exciting." *RT Book Reviews*

"THE THREE FATES OF RYAN LOVE will throw you into a world of mythical proportions with Gods, demons, and seers like you've never dreamed possible. In one word — Amazing!" *Fresh Fiction*

4 1/2 star Top Pick: "Fascinating ...powerful ... beautifully wrought."
RT Book Reviews on The Five Deaths of Roxanne Love

Top Pick: "I absolutely loved The Five Deaths of Roxanne Love, and am eagerly anticipating the next book in the series." *Night Owl Romance*

"A richly developed time-swept paranormal series that should be on every romance lover's shelf."
USA Today Books

THE LONG GONE GIRL
of *Starlight Bend*

ERIN QUINN

CHAPTER ONE

KARI DALE SPOTTED the aptly named *Bar On The Lake* from the street as soon as she pulled into Starlight Bend. It slouched low over the water, supported by thick stilts and a sagging dock. A solid wall of windows reflected the mystical mountains, frigid waters, and the swollen, winter sky surrounding it. To Kari, it looked like a magical place, just for adults. Exactly what she needed after the last hour of white-knuckled driving on icy roads. With a sigh of relief, she parked in the gravel lot and hurried into the sheltered warmth of the bar.

At four p.m. on a random Thursday afternoon, only a scattering of tables had customers, and less than a handful of the barstools had butts in them. Pretending she didn't notice the stares following her, she added her butt to the count, shrugged out of her heavy coat, and looked around.

A fire blazed in a giant stone fireplace behind her, heating the dark, hopsy smells in the air like fragrant oils. Antlers, horns, and dusty old animal heads hung on the other two walls, but it was the breathtaking view that drew her eyes. The floor to ceiling windows looked out at the lake and mountains like a portal into another world.

A graying bartender with a lot of mileage on his lined face slid a cocktail napkin in front of her. "Whatdaya have?" he asked.

"A glass of wine, please. Pinot Noir if you have it."

"I don't."

"Oh. Well, then . . . what reds do you have?"

He hooked a thumb at two nozzled boxes stuffed into a countertop fridge. One box had *White* written across the side, the other *Red*.

"I'll have a beer and a shot, please," Kari corrected.

"Shot of what?"

"Uh...."

"Whiskey?" the bartender prompted.

She'd been thinking more along the lines of a Lemon Drop or a Buttery Nipple, but the look on the bartender's face was enough to stop her from ordering one.

"Yes," she said. "Whiskey."

At the other end of the bar, a man looked up from his red pen and stack of papers. Silvery eyes nearly the same shade as the clouded sky behind him lingered on her for a second too long before he took a drink of what looked like watered down iced tea, and went back to work.

"Any particular kind?" the bartender asked.

"You have choices?"

She thought it a reasonable question, considering his wine selection. Evidently, she was wrong.

"Yes, I have choices," he said hotly. "I got Irish

2

whiskey, Scotch, Canadian, bourbon, rye, single malt—
"

"Quit badgering the woman, Stan," the man at the bar interrupted.

Kari shot him a surprised glance and he returned it with a smile.

"I'll take the Irish whiskey, please," she said, though she wouldn't know Irish whiskey from Canadian, if it stood in a line up with a green sign and a flag.

Stan grumbled as he moved away. He didn't ask her what kind of beer she wanted—that one she could have answered. Instead he drew a Bud Lite from the tap and set it down beside a shot glass filled with amber liquid.

The man at the end of the bar shook his head when Stan moved away. To Kari, he said, "Rough day?"

Day. Week. Year.

"Something like that."

She took a sip of her beer and gave the red pen poised over his papers a curious look.

"High School history," he said after a small pause. "Essays on the Manifest Destiny. I'm not even halfway through grading them and I want to jump off a cliff. Maybe I should start drinking, too."

"Some days you just have to," she agreed, and he smiled again.

It was a nice smile, too. The way it fanned the lines around his eyes and framed his mouth made her think he used it often, and not just in bars with strangers. He didn't look like any teacher she'd ever had, though. Dark hair, light eyes, and a disreputable shadow on his jaw that roughened the edges in the best way. She wondered how many of his female students had crushes on him. Probably all of them.

She'd been staring. Flustered, she picked up her shot and drank it—all at once like she did it all the time. The whiskey was sweet, strong, and smooth as honey, but that didn't stop it from burning her throat and stealing her breath. Only vigorous coughing for what felt like an eternity restored it.

When she finally opened her watery eyes again, the history teacher was watching her with concern and the grouchy bartender looked like he was ready to start pounding her on the back.

"Wrong pipe," she said.

Neither one looked like they believed her, but the teacher seemed relieved that she wasn't about to keel over.

Now that she wasn't gasping, she could feel the heat of the whiskey, warming her from belly to brain. It felt good, cathartic even. She wasn't really the kind of person who went to bars by herself. Pick up a bottle of wine and drink it at home in her PJs? That was more her style. But she'd been working so much lately, pushing herself so hard, that she needed this...whatever this turned out to be.

"I don't think I've ever seen you here before," the teacher spoke again. "Are you new in town or just passing through?"

"Passing through. Eventually."

"You don't like Montana?"

"What I've seen of it is beautiful. I just don't like staying in one place."

"Ever?"

She didn't know how to answer that question. She'd been on the go for so long that it was all she knew. She shrugged, and like the lunatic she was, pushed her shot glass forward with a nod at Stan.

When she looked again, the teacher had turned his attention back to grading his essays. She stared at his bent head, trying to think of something to say next. She felt awkward sitting at the bar all alone. Though the whiskey eased her tension, it didn't fill her with sparkling conversation, unfortunately.

She glanced at the lake view behind him. Earlier it had been raining, then sleeting. Now, fat flakes drifted down.

"Does it always snow this early?" she asked when the man looked up.

"Most years," he answered dryly. "October isn't early, though. August, that's early."

"Wow," she said, nodding, though he hadn't asked a question. "You're from Starlight Bend, then?"

"Born and raised," he said.

"I can't even imagine that. The longest I ever lived in one place was four years—a little town in New Mexico that no one's ever heard of."

The bartender filled her shot glass just as the jukebox began playing *Night Moves*.

"Good song," she said, smiling.

The history teacher studied her for a moment, glanced at her shot glass, and then looked into her eyes. "Are you here to drink alone, or would you like some company?"

He had a nice voice, rich and smooth. Deep down, something gave her a hard elbow in a soft place. *Yes*, it whispered, *she wanted company*. Surprised at the power of the feeling, she nodded.

"Company would be nice."

"You sure?" he asked.

And she liked that he asked. It spoke of a gentleman's manners. Of a confident man who didn't want to push. Or, most likely, didn't need to.

"Yeah," she said, feeling her cheeks heat. "Why not?"

He nodded, picked up his stack of papers, tapped them a couple times to straighten the edges, then crammed them into his satchel. Man, satchel, and the watery iced tea, moved down the bar to the empty seat next to her. The old bartender watched it all suspiciously.

"Stan, I'll have what she's having," he said, pushing the tea forward so Stan could dump it.

"Ain't it a school night?" Stan asked with a sour frown.

The teacher's brows shot up and he grinned. "You gonna call my dad and tell on me?"

"Maybe I will," Stan grumbled, moving to the taps. A few seconds later, he placed the beer and a shot of whiskey on the bar. The teacher clinked his glass against hers before drinking down the shot without coughing his brains out after. He did suck a quick breath through his teeth, though.

"Haven't done that in a while," he said with a laugh.

Cautiously, she took a drink of hers, too, finishing it in a several small swallows this time. The second one went down easier than the first and warmed her blood like wildfire.

"I'm Tyler," the teacher said, holding out his hand. "But everyone calls me Ty."

"I'm Kari. With a K."

She put her hand in his, shocked by its warmth and size. He gave hers a gentle squeeze and released, but didn't pull away. She didn't, either. It was the alcohol, she told herself.

"Welcome to Starlight Bend, Kari with a K."

For a moment, they just stared at one another, still touching. Still not pulling away. Stan muttered something she couldn't make out and finally, she slipped her hand from Ty's. Her palm tingled and she curled her fingers around it to hold onto his warmth.

Ty turned in his seat so he faced her, one booted foot on the railing by her stool. "So . . . what brings you to our little corner of paradise, Kari?"

"The same thing that brought me to this bar," she answered truthfully. "Work."

"You don't like your job?"

"I love my job. I've just been in overdrive lately. I guess I'm a little burned out." A lot burned out, actually, but she was in the homestretch of this sprint. Almost there, if she could just keep it together long enough to reach the finish line.

He nodded with understanding. "Burn out is hard to get past. What kind of work do you do?"

"I co-own a small chain of men's clothing stores," she said. "My business partner and I have opened four so far."

"Impressive. And you're opening another near here?"

"Right here. In Starlight Bend."

Ty let out a bark of laughter. When she didn't join in, his expression turned incredulous. "You're serious?"

"Absolutely. I have just enough time to get the doors open and catch the holiday retail wave."

"Wave? Starlight Bend isn't big enough for a wave."

"Maybe, maybe not. It's an easy drive from Kalispell and not far from the Canadian border, though. Canadians like nice things, right?"

"Sure."

She narrowed her eyes, not trusting that *sure*. "It's a solid location. Our other stores are in similar demographics and they're doing fine."

He took a drink of his beer, eyes glinting again. "Have you ever even been to Montana before, Kari?"

"No, but—"

"*No?*"

"It doesn't matter. We know what we're doing." She might have left it at that, but he looked so unconvinced that she had to go on. "The ratio of men to women is very high in Starlight Bend," she told him. "That's good for sales."

Had she really just said that? Had to be the alcohol. Normally, she was very articulate about their strategic plan and the success they'd had so far. But normally, she wasn't drinking shots in a bar beside a man who looked like this one. Up close, he took attractive to a whole new level.

"And you think that ratio's going to make all the men go shopping?" he asked, clearly perplexed.

"Well, yes. If they want to catch the eye of the fairer sex."

"The fairer sex?" he repeated skeptically. "I hate to tell you this, Kari, but that's not really the way things are done out here."

"Yeah, that's what they said in the last town, and the one before that. But some things are the same no matter where you go. If a man wants to make a good first impression—"

Ty held up a hand. "Sweetheart, in this town, first impressions get made when you're born."

"My point exactly."

"What point?" he said with a teasing laugh that made her smile, too.

"He's going to have to make her look *twice*," she insisted. "The women here know everything about the men in their vicinity. And frankly, they're bored."

"Did you Google that?"

"Starlight Bend has almost twice as many men as

women, yet sixty percent of the single women *of marriageable age*, choose to remain single. That's a majority," she said, in case he'd missed it.

"Who does your math?"

She smiled. "Right now, Irish whiskey."

"In that case . . . Stan, load us up."

"Load us up," she agreed, laughing.

Evidently, Stan didn't see the humor. Scowling, he poured them each another shot, which only made it funnier.

"I don't think he likes us," Kari said.

"He loves *me*," Ty said. "I think it's just you he's got problems with."

The door opened and a gust of cold air came in with two men. "Hey, Ty," one of them called out. The other waved, looking curiously between Kari and Ty.

Ty returned the wave, but angled his body toward Kari, putting an arm over the back of her stool.

"Are they coming this way?" he asked.

Casually, she glanced at the men. "They're thinking about it."

"Lean closer. Act like I'm saying something important."

Trying her hardest to look serious, she nodded intently. "And you think Kim Jong-un is really an alien time traveler? How did I not know that, Ty?"

The two men hesitated a few steps away, then moved to take seats by the window.

"I think you're safe from your friends," she murmured.

"Did you just say Kim Jong-un is an alien time traveler?"

"You put me on the spot," she protested.

"And *that's* what came to you?"

His expression made her laugh again. She liked this history teacher. He was quick to smile, smart. Charming, with just enough worldliness gleaming in his eyes to intrigue her. Make her want to know more about him.

He picked up his shot glass. Dutifully, she did, too.

"All right, Kari. Are we going for blackout drunk or just drunk enough to make poor choices?"

"Definitely poor choices."

"Poor choices it is," he said with slow smile that she felt right down to her high-heeled, fur-lined boots.

And it felt good.

She didn't usually mingle with the natives. Her job demanded that she travel light, literally and figuratively. It was simply easier not to form relationships she'd have to deal with later. But she couldn't even remember the last time she'd had a little fun. Or she'd let a man sit close and flirt with her. Or had *sex*.

She glanced at Ty from beneath her lashes and caught him watching her again. From the heat in his eyes, he'd picked up the gist of her thoughts. Now, awareness filled in the spaces between them. The tension added spice to her buzz. Neither one of them had a ring on their finger; they were both of age. Why not relax and enjoy the night?

The door opened again and five or six people

tromped in, shouting hellos at others already there. Ty's name rang out a few times. He waved, but didn't encourage anyone to come closer. She was glad. She didn't want to share him with anyone else.

"Tell me something else about yourself," he said to her. "Where do you live when you're not passing through?"

She caught her lip with her teeth, worrying it. The question felt personal, though she knew most people would put it in the same class as talk about the weather. But to Kari, it seemed like a gentle pulling back of layers to find what was inside. That worried her. Inside-Kari was nothing like the woman who sat beside him now. Inside-Kari was focused, determined, and very ambitious.

Ty raised his brows.

"I live in Arizona," she finally said. "Downtown Phoenix. My balcony is right above the light rail station. I hear it dinging and clanging first thing in the morning and the last thing at night. But I don't care. It reminds me that I have tracks, too."

He leaned back, looking at her as she spoke. *Listening* to what she said. Not something attractive men in small-town bars usually did. Anywhere, for that matter. Usually, they had a phone in their hand and most of their focus on the screen.

Not this man, though. He made her feel like she had his undivided attention. Had, almost since the moment she'd sat down.

"Where do your tracks go?" he asked. The whiskey

had added a soft rasp to his tone that was sexy as hell.

"Up," she answered. "Up and away."

"Huh," he said. "Interesting trajectory for train tracks."

"I'm all about the interesting."

"I can see that."

Silence fell over the bar as the song changed, a thick quiet heightened by Ty's nearness, by her unexpected yearning to be closer still . . . by the answering gleam in his eyes. More people came into the bar, but neither Kari nor Ty looked their way this time.

Rocking Around the Christmas Tree suddenly blared out of the jukebox and made Kari jump. It ruined the smoky mood that had cocooned the two of them, here in this dark bar with the cold breath of winter misting the windows.

"God damn that woman," Stan muttered under his breath.

"I can hear you, Stan," a female sitting far enough away that she couldn't possibly have heard him, called out.

Kari looked at Ty. Ty moved closer and lowered his voice. "Stan and Marianne play this game every year. Stan's not much for the Christmas spirit. Marianne never takes her tree down."

Kari glanced over her shoulder so she could see the young, black-haired woman laughing with her friends.

"If you don't quit cursing at me, Stan, I'm going to play another one," the woman taunted loudly.

Stan looked like he'd swallowed a lemon. He

flipped her the bird and went back to making drinks while everyone at Marianne's table hooted with laughter.

"I think Stan secretly likes it," Ty said, his lips close to her ear, sending a shiver down her spine.

He sat back and smiled again and Kari got lost in the heat of his gaze. Up close, the color of his eyes was more pewter than gray. A patina that came from adversity and maturity. There was something kindred in those eyes.

And that was not a good thing. She was here for business. Important business. Forgetting reality for a night—sure, she could roll with that. Anything deeper? Disaster. This town was a stepping stone for her, a bridge for her tracks to cross. Not a terminus. Not even a hub. When she left, she didn't want to look back, either.

The thoughts were sobering, but Ty was so intoxicating it counteracted the effect and boosted the whiskey in her system. She felt capable. Bullet proof—perfectly equipped to handle whatever might come of this night with Ty the History Teacher.

He still faced her. She'd turned, and now her knees were between his spread thighs and she could feel the heat of them, framing hers. It would be so easy to lean forward, into him.

He shifted and his right arm came to rest on the bar, sleeve pushed back to reveal muscle and crisp, dark hair. His fingers grazed the soft angora of her sweater when he reached for his glass. The brief touch made her breath catch and her eyes meet his. Caught up in the subtle dance they'd begun, she turned her hand so it brushed against his bare skin. He was so warm and he smelled so good—soap and winter, fresh scents with notes of pine and rain mixed in. She wanted to press her nose to his throat and let those intangible scents take over.

"What about you?" she asked, her voice husky. She couldn't even remember what they'd been talking about. "Have you always been a teacher?"

"No."

"I didn't think so."

"Why?"

"I don't know. Just a feeling I guess."

He gave her that slow smile again, and his left hand brushed the side of her knee. Just a touch, a fleeting caress. Glancing, yet somehow possessive. She felt it everywhere—the heat of it, the promise. There was no denying it. No pretending she wanted to.

"I went the corporate route for a while. Marketing. GM hired me right out of college. I hated Detroit, though. Jumped to Yahoo, loved San Francisco, but . . . ." He shrugged. "Wasn't for me, all those long hours trying to crack some secret code—figure out the magic combination that would pay off. It felt pointless after a while."

"What point were you trying to make?" she asked, completely taken by the matter-of-fact tone, mixed as it was with a slight note of confusion—as if he spoke of some stranger whose actions would forever remain a mystery.

Now, his smile had a shy quality that tipped her over the edge of *charmed* and smack into smitten. "I guess I wanted to make a difference. To someone. Maybe just to myself."

Honesty, unadorned. It resonated within her, waking something that had been dormant for so long she didn't even recognize it. Once upon a time, she'd cared about making a difference, too.

"So you decided to come home and be a teacher?" she asked.

He moved his head side to side. Not a nod, not a shake. "More or less. My dad lives here and I thought if I came back, we might reconnect."

His tone had changed. She might have missed it if she hadn't been paying attention. But Ty had become the center of her focus. His gaze dropped to his empty shot glass.

"And did you?" she asked carefully. "Connect?"

His lips quirked. "I liked it better when we were talking about you."

"Am I getting too personal? I'm sorry. I can back off if . . . ."

He shook his head and leaned in. So did she, closer still. His breath was warm, and whiskey laden, soft against her skin.

"Don't back off."

And her lips almost felt the words.

"Okay."

He touched her forehead with his for a moment and

settled back on his stool. Hot and fluttery feeling, she did the same.

"No, we didn't connect. Haven't." He shrugged. "Call it a work in progress."

Curiosity piqued, she wanted to ask, *Why not?* But despite his words, she felt she traveled taboo lands and pushing wasn't the way to go. Instead, she said, "What about your mom? Is she around?"

His smile became more natural, his body language more at ease.

"My mom lives on Maui and I see her a couple times a year. She's married to a ukulele player."

Surprised, Kari laughed. "Please tell me you know how to play one, too?"

"Only when I wear my grass skirt and hula dance." She laughed again, and Ty grinned at her. "If you don't make me talk about my parents anymore, I might show you later."

Later.

Layered with nuance, the word became a promise that traveled like a current between them. She wanted later. The look Ty gave her said he did, too. The whiskey was still working its magic on her and she'd lost all track of time. While they'd sat and drank, winter night had rushed the windows, turning the view into silver and slate. She and Ty had been talking for hours.

Smiling, Ty took her hand in his, turning it so her palm was against his, fingertips to wrist. The sudden touch startled her. Made her heart thump against her ribs.

"I don't see a ring," he said, touching the third finger on her left hand. "No husband holding down the condo back in Phoenix?"

"No husband. No boyfriend. You?"

"No one."

"Why not?"

"Didn't you mention something about a million men to every single female here?"

"Not exactly, but I don't believe *you* haven't been noticed anyway."

"Maybe there's something wrong with me."

"Maybe there's something wrong with both of us," she answered, intending to sound light and witty. But something throbbed in her voice, betraying her.

Ty laced his fingers with hers and stood, holding her hand and gazing down at her with something undefinable in his eyes. Something she wanted to know, to feel. He stood close, his thighs against her knees, his head down, hers raised, their clasped hands between their bodies. His touch was deliberate. Unexpectedly straightforward. This was no casual caress that might or might not have been accidental. And they both knew it on a deep, sexual level that trumped banter and confidences. It was hard to breathe. Harder still to care as all of her attention narrowed down to his hand, holding hers.

"I think…." he began, but he seemed to get lost as he stared into her eyes.

Welcome to the club. She'd been lost from the start.

18

They stared at each other for an electrifying moment, and then he smiled. A sparkling, mischievous flash of amusement that upended her equilibrium.

Whatever he was thinking, she was in. She liked his wit, the wry glitter in his eyes, the sharp intelligence when he spoke. And running through it all was that deep, *kindred* feeling, rooting inside her, weakening her guard.

"Ty," someone called from the room behind them. "Let the girl breathe. In fact, bring her over here so I can meet her, too."

Still looking in her eyes, Ty asked, "What do you want to do, Kari? Pull up some chairs and meet the rest of the town? Or get out of here? Go for a walk, maybe have dinner. With me?"

"Yes," she said. "The second one. With you."

She lost herself in his gaze for another moment, drawn to him like the tides to the shore. Then something over her shoulder caught his attention and made him look around. He frowned. Kari looked, too, wondering what had put that expression on his face.

The bar had filled up with people. Now, every head was turned their way and Kari and Ty might as well have been standing on a stage.

"Why is everyone watching us?" she asked.

"It's a small town and you're the most exciting thing to walk through the door in . . . well, forever."

"And if I leave with you...."

"Everyone will know."

"Does that bother you?"

"I'm not the one trying to start a business here."

And you are, a voice of reason tried to intercede on the side of sanity. She ignored it. This was a magical place and she didn't have to be responsible Inside-Kari here.

"So you think I should...not come with you?" she asked a little wary.

He shook his head. "That's pretty much the opposite of what I think. But it's up to you. If you want to, you know, play it safe, go your own way. I'll understand."

His eyes glittered with the challenge, and she arched an eyebrow back.

"No," she said softly. "That's not what I want at all. Let's get out of here."

CHAPTER TWO

IT HAD BEEN a long time since Ty Timberlake had picked up a woman in a bar. Anywhere, for that matter. In fact, he'd been flying solo for so long that he'd forgotten the thrill of meeting, of *learning*, someone new. The bone-deep excitement of wondering what might happen next, of trying to create a certain outcome. Like persuading this very beautiful woman to come away with him.

And she'd just said yes. She'd looked him in the eye, and she'd said, *Yes.*

She smiled now as she scooted off her barstool. Her soft blue-green sweater picked up the colors in her hazel eyes and made them glow like jewels. Snug jeans that hugged the curve of her hips were tucked into high heeled boots. The boots looked hard to walk in and wouldn't last two weeks of winter here, but they did look good. Despite the drinks, she seemed steady on her feet. He felt steady, too. Whatever was happening here, it wasn't all about the alcohol.

They stared at each other for an awkward moment, and then a sparkling, playful laugh tipped her eyes at the corners and made him grin. Where had she come from, this gorgeous woman? How had she found her way to Starlight Bend, to him?

Some of his friends—guys he'd known since kindergarten—were still trying to coax him into bring Kari over to their table. He ignored them. Half the town had found an excuse to come to Stan's tonight. Marianne had probably alerted the masses. She worked at the school and couldn't keep anything to herself.

Kari seemed a little flustered by all the attention, but kept her cool as she gathered up the big, overstuffed bag she'd hung on the back of her barstool. Ty finished the last of his beer and tossed a fifty on the bar. He didn't wait for change.

"I'll pay half," Kari said as she shrugged into her coat.

"No, you won't."

He moved behind her to help, standing too close, finding reasons to touch the skin at her nape as he pulled that long, dark rope of silken hair free of the collar. Jesus, she smelled good. She wore a light perfume that had been messing with his head ever since he'd sat down beside her.

"But—"

"Give it up," he said in her ear. "That's how we do things here."

She gazed at him over her shoulder, lifting those eyes he'd been staring into for the past few hours until they met his. The mysteries of the world hid behind the look she gave him. And whatever she was thinking, he was on board with the plan.

"Ready?" he asked.

She hesitated and then blurted. "My last name is Dale. Kari Dale."

"Timberlake."

"Timberlake?" she repeated, surprise in her eyes.

"No, Justin isn't my brother or cousin or monkey's uncle," he said automatically. His students asked him that every year.

"That's not what—"

"Ty, you can't keep her to yourself all night!" Thomas Wheeler hollered.

"The hell I can't," Ty said softly, smiling into her eyes. "It's going to get crazy in here in about five seconds. You ready?"

She nodded and he took her hand, slung his satchel onto his other shoulder, and together they walked past the room full of people not even pretending not to watch them, and right out the front door.

It had stopped snowing, but the stretch of sky over Starlight Bend was a dark and stormy gray that blotted out the stars the town had been named for. Fat with snow and rife with thunder, the clouds menaced and hovered, pressing down, biding their time. The air was so crisp, it felt like a layer of ice coated it. Like it should crackle as they moved through it.

"You hungry?" he asked, still holding Kari's hand as they crossed the street. "We could get something to eat."

"And ruin the whiskey buzz we worked so hard for?" she teased. "What happened to poor choices?"

He should laugh. She'd meant it to be funny. But the cold had cleared his head and he found himself asking, "Is that what this is? What we're doing?"

The sexy smile faltered and her eyes grew wide, alert. Spangled as a fall forest.

"Isn't it?" she asked.

"Unless it's not," he said.

She took a deep breath, nodding quickly. He wasn't sure if that meant agreement or something else entirely.

Her gaze shifted to his mouth and he felt it. He fucking *felt* its heat as it lingered there. Her smile was hesitant as she stepped forward. She settled her palms on his chest and balanced on the balls of her feet, face turned up to his. He groaned when their mouths touched. She tasted of whiskey and woman, a little wild, a little sweet.

He pulled her closer, cursing their coats, damning the streetlight that held them in its glow. He kissed her, just like he'd been thinking of doing since she'd smiled at him for the first time. He hadn't been able to keep his eyes off her.

Her arms went around his neck and she pressed her body down the length of his. His hands slipped inside her coat to her back. He took her weight, swept her right off her feet as he deepened the kiss, taking, giving, dying from how damn good she felt against him, in his arms. His heart was racing. His entire body felt rock hard and he yearned to touch every inch of her, kiss her everywhere.

Sometime between the instant she'd made the

dismaying realization that Stan poured his wine from a box, and the moment when she'd looked in Ty's eyes and said, *Yes . . . with you*, he'd been hooked, and hooked deep.

Damn it.

Slowly, he set her back on her feet, but it took a minute before he could force himself to stop kissing her. She was still on tiptoes, the sweep of her lashes veiling her pretty eyes, a plume of mist on her breath.

"Where are you staying?" he muttered, nuzzling her cheek, breathing in that intoxicating scent.

"Ponderosa Resort," she said, tilting her head so he had better access. "Is it far?"

Ty pulled back. "You are not staying at the Ponderosa," he said emphatically. "I wouldn't let *Stan* stay at Ponderosa."

"Why?" she asked, blinking. "The pictures on their website looked nice and it's only for the night. Tomorrow, I'm moving into a rental house."

Ty shook his head. "The roaches don't even like the Ponderosa, Kari."

"No," she breathed in horror.

"Afraid so, sweetheart. You can stay with me. No strings. I even have a spare room. Clean sheets."

She didn't say anything and he couldn't tell what she was thinking. Great romancer that he was, he'd introduced cockroaches and spare rooms into a perfect moment. Now she was probably thinking of getting out of town as fast as she could.

"Neither one of us should be driving anyway."

He just kept talking. She no longer had that hungry look in her eyes.

"Or we could call a cab, go someplace else. It'd be coming from Kalispell, though. If it comes at all."

It was like a sickness. A can't-shut-up sickness.

Kari's lips quirked in a smile she couldn't seem to hide.

She caught his jacket in her hands and tugged. He obliged by bending down as she came up on tiptoes again—Jesus, that was sexy—her mouth hot against his. His hand tunneled beneath the warm weight of her hair and he cupped the back of her head, lost in the feel of her lips, her tongue, her taste. Who cared about tomorrow when he had her in his arms right now? Her skin was so soft that once he touched it, he couldn't stop. The silky line of her jaw, the vulnerable curve of her throat, the satiny stretch over hollow and bone just above the neckline of her sweater.

He couldn't think anymore, not when all the blood in his body had gone south.

He took a deep breath, forced himself to slow down. Reluctantly, he eased back and waited for her to open her eyes. See him. Her lashes fluttered over honey and hazel before her gaze focused on him.

They were still standing in front of Stan's. Hell, they'd been making out in the center of town. Mrs. Paxton had probably already posted pictures of them on Facebook.

"How many shots did we do?" he asked.

"What?" she said, surprised. Then, "Three . . .

maybe four. Is that a test? You want me to walk a line?"

How did she make that sound so tempting?

He smiled at her. "Sure. Let's see it."

She held out her arms, wobbled once, then found her center. She toe-heeled for a few feet while he admired the view, then turned and came back.

"I'm feeling good, Ty. But I'm not drunk. I know what I'm doing."

"Yeah?" he said, kissing her again, because he couldn't help himself. "And what is that exactly?"

"I'm going home with you."

God help him. Every cell in his body heard that.

"I mean . . . if you want me, too."

"Yeah, I want. Just making sure the cold air didn't wake you up. Maybe change your mind."

"It didn't. I haven't."

"Okay," and because the way she looked at him made him feel like Superman, he scooped her up in his arms and started walking while she laughed and kissed his neck, his face. When she reached his mouth, he had to stop and just hold her while she drove him to the edge.

"How far?" she whispered in his ear.

Just up the street and around the corner. A half-mile, if that.

"Too damned far."

"Put me down. We'll get there faster."

They walked the quiet street holding hands, saying nothing as their footsteps echoed on the pavement. He

27

didn't know what time it was. Maybe eight, maybe midnight. The frosted dark made it hard to tell. The tension inside him made it hard to care. The need to get her alone, consumed him.

They stepped through the front door and his little dog poked her head out of the kitchen to bark hello.

"That's Buttercup," he told Kari as he knelt to greet the Beagle. "For the record, my students named her, not me."

"She's so cute," Kari said, getting down on her knees beside him. "Hi, Buttercup."

Tail wagging, Buttercup belly-crawled up to them, then rolled on her back in total submission.

"I found her out by the lake last spring. Freezing, starving. No tags. She was pretty beat up. I don't know what she tangled with, but it had claws. I posted ads, but no one ever claimed her."

"How can that be?" she asked Buttercup, gently scratching her tender underbelly and stroking her sides.

"She's usually pretty shy."

"So am I," Kari told the dog. "You should try whiskey. It helps."

Ty laughed. "Let me give her a treat and put her to bed."

Kari shed her coat as he took Buttercup out to the backyard, then gave her a bedtime cookie. Her bed was under the kitchen table.

"That's where she sleeps?" Kari asked, leaning against the doorframe.

"I guess it makes her feel safe. I tried putting her

bed in other rooms, but she always ends up back here."

"Silly Buttercup. You should climb in bed with him," Kari said. "He'll keep you safe."

Jesus, was there anything about this woman that didn't turn him on?

He switched off the kitchen light and caught Kari up in his arms, turning her against the wall, pressing close. She shoved his jacket off his shoulders and it hit the ground. His hands were under her sweater, hers at the buttons of his shirt. Her face was turned up to his, her eyes bright in the shadows. She finished undoing his last button then lifted her arms so he could slide her sweater over her head. He tossed it on the floor. His flannel and undershirt followed.

He wanted her body against his, but she was lovely standing there in the muted light, her skin ivory smooth and satin soft. For a moment, all he could do was stare. A plain white bra covered her full breasts, holding them high. Gently he grazed his fingertips over the soft flesh, then cupped them in his hands. She was curved in all the right places, soft as only a woman could be, and so very beautiful. Kari arched into his touch and made a sound that awakened everything male inside him.

He was so hard it hurt.

Her fingers were icy against his hot skin when she reached for the top button of his jeans, then into his pants. Shocking, incredible. His head fell back, and his knees gave a mighty wobble.

"Christ . . . Kari . . . ."

Her hands were all over him now, sensuous chaos

that shredded his thoughts, laying waste to his plan of seduction. There was only Kari, how she felt in his arms, against his lips, deep down on levels that couldn't sustain thinking.

If he didn't take control, this would be over before it started. And that was the last thing he wanted.

He caught her wrists and pinned them over her head as he pressed his body to hers. Their chests heaved in tandem, their breath, hot and fast. She made another sound in her throat that resonated beneath the skin, to the very core of him.

He covered her mouth with his, wanting that sound again, wanting to taste it, feel it against his tongue. The kiss was deep, drugging, an addiction he'd never stop craving. Her hips rocked—oh, so slightly—but his body understood the rhythm and mirrored it. He felt all-powerful when he lifted her and she hooked those shapely legs around him, boot heels at the small of his back, arms twined at his neck, mouth still hot and urgent on his. She wrapped herself around him like moonlight and he soaked it in, soaked it up.

He carried her to his bedroom and laid her on his bed. She'd said she had tracks that would take her up and away. Maybe she did. But tonight she was his.

CHAPTER THREE

THE SURPRISE ACTUALLY surprised Ty the next morning. When he'd fallen asleep, Kari had been in bed beside him, warm and naked and soft as a dream. She was long gone when he'd woken up, though. Not unexpected. She'd been clear that *staying* was not her thing. Still, he hadn't expected her to bolt.

Sometime after one, he figured. She'd still been there at midnight when he'd rolled over and pulled her close to make love to her one more time. And she'd been willing, passionate . . . as into him as he was to her. At least, that's what he'd thought.

He padded into the kitchen, stopping to pet Buttercup who gazed at him with big, sympathetic eyes. She knew all about waking up abandoned.

"Did you happen to see a beautiful naked woman come through here this morning?" he asked her.

Buttercup wagged her tail and turned in a circle at his feet.

"You did, huh? Why didn't you try to stop her?"

Kari had left a note on the kitchen table. He could picture her writing it, bra stuffed in her purse because she'd dressed quickly in the dark, hoping he wouldn't wake up. No shoes, feet cold on the tile. Hair, a glorious mess.

The note read, *Had to run. Kari.*

Coward. She'd taken off rather than face the reality of waking up with a stranger who'd had his hands and mouth over every inch of her body. He smiled. The memory was that sweet.

He picked up his phone, found the number for the Ponderosa and called.

"Sue Bee," he said when Sue Bee Chen answered. Her family had owned the Ponderosa almost as long as his had owned Timberlake Hardware store. That didn't mean she kept the place up, though. Sue Bee liked to gamble and any profit she might have made went along the lines of her inheritance—straight to the casino.

"This is Ty Timberlake. Is there a woman by the name of Kari Dale staying in one of your rooms?"

"Did you tell her we have roaches?" Sue Bee demanded.

"I—"

"Did you?"

"Is she there?"

"No. She paid one night and went somewhere else to stay. Someone told her about the roaches. I know it."

"Did she say where she was going?"

"What do I care?" She can go to—"

"Did she?"

Sue Bee sighed with irritation. "A Hilton," she sneered. "That's what she said. *Points.*"

Like it was a dirty word.

There were only two Hiltons within a hundred miles of Starlight Bend. That was a lot of distance to cover in the dark, over unfamiliar, probably icy roads. He'd been stone-cold sober by the time he'd wrapped his body around hers and gone to sleep. He was willing to bet that she'd been, too. Still.

He tried the closest Hilton first—the one near Glacier Park—and when he asked for "Kari Dale's room," was instantly told to hold while his call was transferred to her room.

He hung up before it rang. She'd checked in, made it there safe. That's all he needed to know.

But it really wasn't. Not even close.

Neither the crisp morning nor his walk with Buttercup dispelled his foul mood. He dressed for work and headed to the Lakeside Café for some breakfast. There was zero chance that word hadn't already spread about him leaving with Kari last night. Best to face the razing that waited for him head on and get it over with.

The Lakeside Café was just around the corner from Stan's and the scent of roasting coffee beans guided him like a beacon. The roaster sat right in the front and on cold days like this, the smell of coffee and cinnamon filled the streets.

It was barely seven in the morning when Ty walked in and the place was already packed. Luckily, he found an empty stool at the counter.

"You look like hell this morning, Romeo," Becky, the café owner, teased as she poured him a cup of coffee.

He flashed a smile, like the teasing didn't bother him, and wrapped his hands around the mug.

"That woman wear you out, did she?" a male voice asked from a few seats down. Ty leaned forward and caught sight of Andy, the town's MacGyver, sitting there. Andy hadn't been at the bar last night, but Thomas sat right next to him, and had probably blabbed about it.

And joy of joys, Ty's dad sat on his left.

Henry Timberlake looked as hale and hearty as he had twenty years ago, but after mom had left him, he'd shriveled up on the inside, where no one could see. No one but his son, that is.

"Dad," Ty said with a nod.

"Son," Henry answered stiffly.

That was about as deep as their conversations went these days. It hadn't taken long for Ty to realize that coming back home to reconnect had been a fool's mission. In Henry's mind, leaving in the first place had been an unforgiveable crime.

"Heard about your shenanigans with some woman who blew into town," Henry went on, speaking over Andy.

Ty thought before he answered. Anything he said could and would be used against him.

"No shenanigans," he said at last. "Just drinks."

"She went home with you," Henry accused.

Yeah, and thanks for announcing it to everyone, pops.

"Only because she was staying at the Ponderosa."

A collective gasp came from all around them. Even Becky stopped her bustling to grimace.

"I couldn't let her go there," Ty finished.

"No," Thomas agreed enthusiastically. "Hell, no."

"How long is she in town?" Andy wanted to know.

Ty shrugged. "You'd have to ask her."

"She'll be here for a time," Henry said knowingly.

"Why's that?" Stan asked.

"Well, if her name is Kari Dale, she bought the hardware store last week. Her and another gal. Business partners."

Ty stared at his father, so confused he didn't know where to start. He knew Kari? She'd *bought* the hardware store? He'd *sold* the hardware store that had been in their family for over two hundred years?

"What—wait. You sold the store? To . . . Kari?"

He couldn't wrap his mind around it. The woman who'd breezed into town and his bed last night, had just . . . *bought* his unwanted legacy? How could that even have happened? She said she owned clothing stores . . . right?

"But . . . when? How . . . *why?*" He looked into his father's eyes, and saw every wrinkle formed from pain and loss. Without the store, Henry was . . . . "It was your life blood, Dad. I thought—"

"What'd you think, son?" The word was almost a taunt. "That I'd give it to you?"

"No, I thought you'd keep—"

"For what? For who? A son who walks away when the going gets tough?"

Ty's ears rang. His cheeks flushed. Same old conversation. Same old anger. Same old dad, clinging to a false sense of betrayal. Ty was sick of it. But not sick enough to stop it. Not yet, anyway.

His father stood, throwing down some money on the counter. "You didn't care enough about it to make a difference when you could have. You got no place in it now."

Everyone was watching them. People he'd known most of his life. People who'd thought him selfish to have left when his family needed him. People who understood that he'd had to go. And mixed in, people like his dad who thought he shouldn't have bothered to come back.

A cold gust rushed into the taut silence as the front door opened. Ty saw it as a reprieve and looked away from his dad's resentful face. Henry muttered something under his breath and showed himself to the door just as Kari walked in. Henry was too wrapped up in himself to notice. He didn't even look up as he brushed past her, but everyone else took note of the woman stepping aside to get out of his way.

Kari looked like something out of Hollywood with her silky fall of dark hair, her expensive coat and fancy boots. She had big eyes, earthy and colorful, framed by dark lashes and a creamy complexion. Her gaze skittered over the curious faces turned her way until it found his and stuck. Color washed over her cheeks and down the smooth line of her throat. For a moment, she looked like she might bolt.

Again.

"We don't have any tables," Chelsea, the teenager working the register, told Kari. "If you give a me a sec, I'll clear that place at the counter."

Kari blinked at her, as if trying to understand the words. "Uh, no. I don't want to . . . . May I have a cup of coffee to go, please? Biggest cup you have."

"Sure."

Ty felt like there was a stone lodged up high under his breastbone. He knew it for what it was—fury. He was angry with his father, for the messed up excuse of a relationship they had. But some of that anger belonged to this woman, who'd fled his house in the dark without even a goodbye. Who'd bought Timberlake Hardware—*why*, Ty couldn't begin to fathom. Who stood there looking so damn pretty that even now he wanted to sweep her off her feet and make them both forget why he was mad.

Deliberately, he stood. Kari saw him moving toward her and her eyes went wider and rounder, her flush darkened. He could smell her perfume as he drew near and a rush of memory nearly did him in.

"Good morning," he said to Kari, like he wasn't coming undone.

"Good morning," she said softly.

Her gaze found his again. She looked like she wanted to say something. A part of him wanted to hear it, but a part of him had just been tipped over a very steep ledge. He didn't want to hear anything else. Not from her, not from his dad, not from anyone.

Making the decision for them both, he reached past Kari and handed Chelsea a ten. "I had a coffee. I'll buy hers, too."

"You don't—" Kari began.

Ty cut her off with a look. "I know. It's just how we do things here."

She blushed again and looked down. And even though it made no sense at all, Ty felt like an ass.

Coffee was cheap at Becky's. Chelsea rang him up and handed him a five in change. He stuffed it in her tip jar and said, "Make good choices today."

Behind him Kari sucked in a breath.

And then he was gone, out into the fresh air, thinking that yesterday his biggest concern had been grading crappy papers. Overnight, everything had changed and now it felt like his world had been turned upside down.

CHAPTER FOUR

NUMB, KARI WATCHED Ty leave the café. He'd been angry—she could see it. She didn't even blame him for being mad at her. *She* was mad at herself. But there'd been something else in his eyes, something that told her his anger hadn't been solely directed at her.

"Here you go," the cute teenager behind the cash register interrupted Kari's thoughts, holding out a large cup of coffee that Kari knew wouldn't be anywhere near big enough.

Only when she was back in her car, sealed inside and all alone, did she let loose the string of curse words that had been lodged in her throat since Ty's eyes had met hers across the café.

She finished her creative litany with a dependable, "*Damn it*," shouted at her steering wheel. That wasn't enough though. She *thunked* her head against it a couple of times, too.

She'd been second guessing herself since she'd tiptoed out of Ty's bedroom last night and dressed in the kitchen—in the dark, boots in her hand and her bra stuffed in her purse, like some hoochie mama on TV.

But reality had forced its way into her bliss as she

laid beside Ty, listening to his even breathing, snuggled to the warmth of his hard body. Making love with him had literally blown her mind. She'd never been with a man who took his time, who gave so much. Even in sleep, he surrounded her with his body and made her feel safe and protected.

That's what had set her off. That comfortable, secure, *settled* feeling.

Kari had been on her own since she was eighteen. She answered to no one and she relied only on herself. She had things to do, places to be, and no room in her life for a man, especially one as all-consuming as Ty Timberlake.

So she'd run. Cowardly, yes. But very effective.

Only now that voice in her head wouldn't shut up about it. About how amazing it had felt to cut loose, to be nothing more than a woman having a good time with an attractive man. A *very* attractive man. That voice kept nagging, telling her she'd run from something that might have been good if she'd given it a chance.

"Why didn't you say something to him?" she said aloud, meeting her own gaze in the rearview mirror. Instead, she'd just stood there in the café like an idiot, staring at him and not saying a damn thing. He either thought she was a lunatic or a bitch. Probably both.

She *thunked* her head on the steering wheel again, but it didn't change anything. It certainly didn't make it better. Finally, she started her car. She had a lot to do today. Everyday. She didn't have time for regrets.

Yet she couldn't stop feeling them either.

Sighing, she mapped the address of her rental on her cell phone, took a quick drink of coffee, closing her eyes when the delicious brew hit her taste buds and warmed her belly, then she put the car into drive and headed *home.*

The small house—cabin, really—had come furnished, sorta. The couch was relatively new, if ugly as hell, and the kitchen was stocked with pots, pans and dishes. A small dinette provided a place to eat, though usually she ate in front of the television, watching HGTV with a glass of wine and her laptop.

She'd done this small town thing enough times to know what to expect in a rental. The day she'd signed the lease, she'd arranged for a satellite dish, wireless Internet, two new fire extinguishers, a new bed, and a professional cleaner.

Before unpacking, she tucked one of the extinguishers under the kitchen sink, the other in the bedroom. Next, she hung her calendar on the kitchen wall where she could see it first thing in the morning. The days between now and her eminent departure on January eighth were numbered in a countdown. Seventy-two days to go.

On day seventy-three, Kari would start visiting potential locations for their next store. Usually, she looked forward to that. But Starlight Bend marked the fifth store in as many years and she was tired. Only her faith in the business plan that she and her partner, Simone, had meticulously created, kept her going.

But the wild night in the bar on a lake with a man

she couldn't stop thinking about had filled her head with thoughts of a different kind of life. One that came with a slower pace. Less work, more laughter. She'd never achieve her goals that way, though. And goals were important. She hadn't busted her ass for the past five years only to quit when she was almost there. Especially not for a man.

The stern talking-to sustained her for the rest of the day. But when she finally went to sleep that night, Ty was back in her thoughts. Sadly, though, not in her bed.

CHAPTER FIVE

As THEY HAD in every other town, Kari and Simone had purchased the struggling, local hardware store. Home Depot and Lowes had put most of them out of business already, so they came cheap and were surprisingly easy to find. More than that, hardware went with their brand of men's clothing: HardWear. They'd discovered by accident that coupling the old brick and mortar hardware stores with the trendy style of their clothing line created a cool vibe that customers responded to. After that, they'd made the stores part of their branding.

But this time, it was Timberlake's Hardware Store. *Timberlake's.* As in Ty Timberlake? Or was it a common name in this part of the country? Henry Timberlake had signed the escrow papers, but now she had to wonder if maybe Henry was the dad Ty had come home to connect with. What were the odds of that being the case? Did it matter? She'd killed the spark that had glowed between them when she'd run away.

Why did you do that, Kari?

The gong of the cowbell that hung over the hardware store's door saved her from having to answer herself. She must have forgotten to lock it after Simone, her business partner, had left. Thinking Simone had returned for something, she looked up from where she knelt on the floor, the torso of a mannequin between her spread thighs as she tried to slide a pair of skinny jeans over its plastic hips. She'd worked up a sweat and the gust of cold, damp air that rushed in felt good against her skin. She couldn't see over the racks, so she looked under and caught sight of blue jeans that ended in a pair of scuffed boots.

She knew those boots. She'd helped their owner out of them not so long ago.

A second later, long, lean, Ty Timberlake came around the racks and spotted her on the floor. His gaze moved between the half-naked mannequin and her flushed face. He almost smiled.

"Am I interrupting?"

"Uh," she said, scrambling to her feet. It was all she could manage. The sight of him had literally made her breathless. He was even more attractive than she'd remembered. How was that possible?

The day had been filled with manual labor and Kari was sweaty, dirty, and probably smelled. So yeah, perfect time for him to show up.

"What are you doing here?" she asked.

"Looking for you."

"Why?"

She'd meant, *Why, when I was such an idiot to leave your bed in the dead of night?* But the rest of it caught in her throat.

In the days since she'd last seen him, she'd accepted

the dismal fact that nothing more would ever happen between them. She'd even managed to talk herself into thinking it was a good thing. *Moving on. Tracks. Travel light, no baggage.* All the usual reasons she used to keep her distance.

But now that he was here, she could only think of his kisses, his teasing smile, that crisp scent that had tantalized her until she finally had him naked and her nose against his skin.

"The store looks good," he said casually, but his gaze never left her face, watching her reactions, making her feel like he knew what she was thinking. She remembered that, too. He'd seemed so tuned into her, so in synch with her thoughts. "I like the new floors. The walls are a nice color, too."

A hired crew had been out earlier that week to paint and replace the yellowed, peeling linoleum with laminate flooring in a cool ash gray.

"The paint's the original shade," she said, like it mattered. Like anything mattered but the fast rhythm of her heartbeat and the fact that he was here. Here looking for *her*, he'd said. "It still smells like fertilizer, though."

"Always has."

He'd had that same note in his voice when he'd spoken of his father that night in the bar. Not so much sad as it was resigned, stoic.

"I didn't know that I'd bought your father's store," she blurted. "When we met, I didn't know. I mean, I wasn't even sure until just now."

He nodded. "After I calmed down a bit, I figured that out. For the record, I didn't know he'd even sold it. Not until he told me the other morning at the café."

She remembered Ty's anger and the inexplicable certainty that it wasn't just for her. "But hasn't this store been in your family for a long time?"

Ty shoved his hands in his pockets and nodded again. "My great-great-granddad and his brother opened it back in the days of the gold rush. Made their fortune selling bullets and axes to miners."

"Bullets and axes?" she said surprised. "Not shovels and picks?"

"Those, too. But it was the bullets that made their fortune."

They'd kept a few bits of the original decorations—a tin sign for chewing tobacco, a giant ax, an old cash register, and a framed box of bullets. She'd wondered about the bullets. Now it made sense.

"Are you upset with him, for selling?" she asked carefully.

He gave her another half-smile. "I haven't decided. As he's quick to point out, I never had much interest in this store. But it's part of my heritage. A bigger part of his. I'm not sure what motivated him to get rid of it. Spite, maybe. But that always backfires."

She listened solemnly. Obviously, his plan to connect with his father wasn't going well. She wanted to give him a hug. A few nights ago, it would have been easy.

He studied her for a moment, but she had no idea

what he might be thinking. She hoped he was feeling the same way about her.

Finally, he asked, "Why Timberlake's? Why not the abandoned fabric store on the corner? Or the old bank building down the street. That one has more room."

"We always choose a hardware store," she answered. "Our brand name is HardWear—W-e-a-r. Rugged, but stylish fashion."

"Huh," he said, less than impressed.

There'd been a whole lot of unbelievers along the way, but it stung that he was among them.

He turned and wandered a few steps into the store, pensively perusing his family legacy, now stripped down and reengineered into something completely different. He came to a stop in front of the original Timberlake Hardware sign, which Kari had been thrilled to save, even though the lights in the *E* flickered sometimes. They'd hung it on the wall behind the old cash register.

"That started shorting out about twenty years ago. Dad never could find what makes it blink. It drove him nuts." Silently, he stared at the sign, his expression giving little away.

Kari waited, filled with uncertainty. He said he'd come looking for her, but she still didn't know why. All the things that had been left unsaid between them seemed to fill the room, creating invisible barriers that could trip her up at any moment.

"What's that on the phone?" he asked, eyeing the

flashing light clipped to its side.

It was one of her father's inventions. An alarm that—in theory—worked with the smoke detectors to provide an early fire alert.

"A gadget my dad came up with. It probably doesn't even work."

Ty nodded, saying nothing. But just as he had at the bar, he seemed tuned-in to her feelings. Ty Timberlake was a man who paid attention.

Kari turned away before he saw too much and Ty went back to studying the sign.

"I'm not really good at this kind of thing," he said at last. His back was turned to her and she wasn't sure what they were talking about anymore.

"What kind of thing is that?" she asked.

"Hooking up with a woman I've just met. Waking up and finding her gone in the morning."

Oh. That.

"I understand, sometimes bailing is the best option," he went on, still not facing her. "And you did warn me that you don't like staying in one place. But I don't know what comes next, Kari. Do we pretend it didn't happen?"

No, she didn't say.

"Or figure out to how make it happen again?"

Finally, he turned and caught Kari in that quicksilver gaze that saw everything. Like the flash of excitement she was sure had flared in her eyes at the thought of *again*, or the worry that *again* would only lead to disaster. Because truly, that was the root of the problem, wasn't it? Ty had been captivated by the woman he'd met in that bar. But she wasn't real. She'd been make-believe, something Kari wished she could be. The real Kari was here now, though. The one that worked eighteen hours a day, trying to make a mark in a world where everyone else seemed to be brighter and better equipped.

"What do you think we should do?" she heard herself ask.

The corner of his mouth twitched in a smile. "I think we should go to dinner."

The last time he'd invited her to dinner, she'd thrown herself in his arms and hadn't let go until he took her to his bed. Just thinking about it made her feel hot and jittery. But not just that. It scared her. Even when she'd been pretend-Kari, the woman who only cared about having fun, she'd been scared. Ty saw too much. And as twisted and wrong as it was, she liked that he thought of her as that carefree person who drank whiskey and laughed freely and flirted outrageously in dark bars. She didn't want him to know the real Kari. He wouldn't have come looking for *her*.

She glanced down at her grubby self and shook her head. She'd kicked off her shoes hours ago and just had thick socks on her feet. Without her heels, she felt small, vulnerable.

"Okay," Ty said. "Maybe dinner's a bad idea. But I'm a little lost here. I don't understand what happened, why you left like you did. Is it me? Something I said? Something I did? Say so if it is."

Because that's how things worked in his open, honest world.

"It's not you, Ty. It's me. I told you, as soon as the holidays are over, I'll be moving on. Getting involved with you wouldn't be fair."

"So it's my feelings we're worried about?"

"Not just yours," she said softly.

"You afraid you're gonna fall head over heels for me and want to stay?"

Maybe.

Probably.

Okay, yes. And absolutely, she was afraid. She'd spent one night with him and hadn't been the same since. What would she be after a week? *Who* would she be after month? And what if he changed his mind as soon as he realized she wasn't the same girl he'd met in that bar, not on the inside?

"I just don't want any hard feelings when I leave," she said. Convincingly, too. "And that's my plan. To leave. January eighth. It's on my calendar."

"Well, if it's on your calendar . . . ." he said, smiling. "But you're here now and by my count, we have what? Sixty? Seventy, long, cold nights before you go? Seems a shame to waste them."

A smile curved his lips, but the look in his eyes . . . that was serious. He wanted her. He wanted to be with her. And he wanted it enough that he'd come looking for her when she'd run away. Only a fool wouldn't be scared of that. He made her feel like she was on a rollercoaster, only there were no safety belts, no operator, no emergency *Off* switch.   Just dizzying heights and plunging free falls.

But if she let him walk away . . . . She shook her head again.   She didn't even think she *could* let him walk away.

"There's still a kitchen in the back," she said. "Your dad even left the fridge and the table and chairs."

He cocked his head, trying to follow those words to their source. "You feel like cooking?"

That made her smile.   "I only cook for people I don't like."

His brows shot up. "So you do like me.   Against your will—I can see that."

And now she was laughing.   This was such a bad idea.

"I was thinking we could order a pizza.   I could be done with Joaquin—" She pointed at the mannequin on the floor, "—by the time it gets here."

"Joaquin?"

"We're friends.   Don't judge me."

"I wouldn't dream of it.   Pizza sounds like a great plan, but there's no place that delivers in Starlight Bend. I could pick one up, though, while you and Joaquin finish your business.   Bring it back.   Maybe some wine, too?"

"I like all those words.   I have a bottle of wine in the back, though.   We could share it."

"That works."

Like a puppy, she followed him to the door, watched him turn the collar of his sheepskin lined jean jacket up and step into the freezing cold. The air here already smelled of winter, and she swore that Christmas music was always playing somewhere. *Santa Baby* drifted on the crisp air, even now.

Ty stopped and looked back at her. "Don't go anywhere," he said.

And then he was striding down the street, long legs, broad shoulders and perfect behind. Like the fool she was, Kari watched him until the shadows gobbled him up.

CHAPTER SIX

IN A DAZE, Kari dressed Joaquin, fighting stiff limbs and unbendable body parts to get pants, shirts and shoes on him, before manhandling the plastic hipster into the display window. She was out of breath and sweaty again by the time she finished. Ty would be back any minute now, and she probably smelled like she'd been herding cattle all day.

In addition to the kitchen, the shop had a small bathroom in the back. Nervous, excited, *thrilled*, she snagged a clean t-shirt from the stock and wasted no time washing up and doing what damage control she could with her limited supplies.

A glass of wine calmed her down a little. She was sipping, though. She wanted a clear head. No more poor choices if she could help it.

Problem was, she didn't think she could.

The cow bell gonged a moment before Ty walked in again, pizza box balanced in his right hand, a six pack under his arm, and a bottle of wine gripped by the neck in his other hand. He set everything on the table, then paused, waiting until she looked at him.

"Second thoughts?" he asked.

She smiled, feeling unbelievably shy. "No."

He shrugged out of his coat and draped it over the back of the chair, snagged a beer and opened the pizza box.

"In that case, I give you, Pizza Frank," he said.

"Pizza *Frank?*"

Ty nodded sagely. "Trust me. He's a genius."

And once again, he turned on the charm, making her laugh. Making her feel funny, too. The pizza was amazing, but it paled compared to the company. All the hollow hurt that had filled her this past few days began to dissipate as she relaxed and enjoyed herself.

Her glass of wine was empty and she wanted another, but didn't pour it and shook her head when Ty offered. He still nursed his first beer.

"So," he said softly after they'd both finished. "This calendar of yours. It's set in stone?"

"Kind of," she said, wary. "Once we get through the launch of this store, I'll be looking for the site of the next one."

"Building an empire?"

"Not really. It's more about proving I can turn straw into gold."

His brows went up in surprise. "Okay. Why?"

She let out a deep breath. There was so many ways to answer that, but in the end, it really came down to her dad. "My father was an inventor. Everything he saw, every day of his life, he was thinking of how he could fix it. Make it better. More efficient. Some of his ideas were shit—I won't kid you—but every once in a while, he'd come up with something genius."

"Like?"

"eReaders."

Ty looked shocked. "Your dad invented eReaders?"

"Yes. Does he hold the patent? No. His prototype is in a pile of junk somewhere, along with a hundred other prototypes—electric potato peelers and rotating shower heads. My personal favorite? Vibrating alarm clock pillows—the gentle waker-uppers."

"What happened to those?"

"Eight out of ten people fell into a deeper sleep when the pillows started vibrating."

"No shit?"

"Right? He had so many ideas that he couldn't tell the good from the bad—hence the eReader tragedy. Before Sony, before Kindle, before all of them, he had a working model, but he threw it in the junk pile and moved on."

"That's still pretty impressive."

"Sad, is more like it. Which is why I don't want to follow in his footsteps."

She fiddled with a piece of crust on her paper plate, not looking at him. She didn't talk about her dad, hadn't for years.

"What do you do instead?" he asked.

"I succeed," she answered.

"Lucky you," he said, totally at ease, which was precisely *not* how she was feeling, despite Pizza Frank and the glass of wine. Tension knotted her shoulders and she could feel her brow furrowing. She tried to smooth it out. She was not a fan of conversations about failure. Or a fan of *anything* about failure.

"Oh, I've had my share of false starts, too," she said, brushing her hair back with her fingers. "But that's because I take risks and stay focused. Believe it or not, this is one of the safer ventures."

"What were the others?"

She gave him a wry smile and held up a finger. "First, there were Planterns."

"What are they?"

"Flammable, as it turns out. Just like the trees they were supposed to hang in. Thank God for insurance."

He grinned, obviously picturing *that* debacle.

"Okay. What else?"

"I sold knockoff designer purses for a while. That was lucrative, but not sustainable. Too many customs issues, trying to get them in the country. Then the factory I was using burned down. I took it as a sign."

"Stay away from fire?"

She stared at him, startled—not many people joked about burnt-out factories. She wasn't sure how to react to it. It had been a monumental disaster, a crater in the middle of her road she almost hadn't gotten around.

"It wasn't funny," she said indignantly.

"Sorry," he answered, not looking sorry at all. In fact, he was having a hard time keeping the smile off his face.

"You don't seem too shocked by all my failures," she said, mystified.

"I'm shocked that you haven't invested in fire extinguishers yet."

This time, she laughed, too, and the tension flowed out of her. "Oh, trust me, I have. They're strategically placed in every one of our stores, including this one, *and* my house. I even have one in the car."

He was still grinning when he got up to throw their plates away.

"So after your purse business went up in flames?"

"It took me awhile, but I was able to sock away enough money to buy into this. *This*," she said, gesturing at the store, "is working. It's a slow return on investment, but it's building. We're so close to making it, I can feel it."

"And then what?"

"We sell and move on."

"To?"

"The next big thing, whatever it is. That's how fortunes are made."

He took his seat at the table again. "Why small town hardware stores, though? I mean, I get the connection to your brand, but it seems like you're limiting your potential, moving into low population areas—even if the ratio of men to women is a trillion to one."

She rolled her eyes at his exaggeration.

"Men's fashion is a four-hundred-billion-dollar industry. To get a brand in Leimann's, Nordstrom's, or even a store like Kohl's, there has to be a track record. We didn't have the money to open up in multiple malls—which is what it would have taken to get noticed—but a small town like this? We could afford to start up right away. The competition is scarce and we're the biggest fish in a tiny little pond. We're pretty much the *only* fish."

"The only fish, without a lot of fish food."

"See, that's where you're wrong," she said, warming to the subject, forgetting for the moment that he didn't know this calculating, unsexy side of her. "There's also the element of exclusivity. You can't just buy our products anywhere."

"And that's a good thing? You're not online?"

"Not yet. We need to build a demand first. People want what they can't have. The harder it is to get, the more they want it."

"And the more they'll pay to get it. Smart," he said, and she felt a warm flush at his approval. "So how are you going to accelerate that return on investment?"

"This is the fifth store. The others are turning a marginal profit, but we need a splash. Something that puts us on the radar and draws in a major buyer. It could be this store—or it might be the next one. But like I said, we're close. I feel it in my gut."

"And this splash? How are you going to make that happen?"

She puffed out some air and shook her head. "I'm working on it."

And by working on it, she meant trying frantically to figure out something that would break them out of the pack. Searching out the trendiest fashions, always pushing the envelope on what they stocked. Staying in touch with designers and buyers overseas, while at the same time, mining sites like Etsy for that new, undiscovered "voice" that would define what men wore tomorrow. That's where they found the designers who were as hungry to be discovered as Kari and Simone were to make it big.

"And that's what it's all about for you? Cashing out and moving on?"

When he said it, this golden dream that had kept her going sounded very tarnished. Hollow. At the same time, cashing out and moving on was liberating. Cleansing in a way he'd probably never understand.

"It is right now," she answered, not meeting his eyes.

He nodded, contemplative as he toyed with his beer bottle, saying nothing. She wanted to ask about his past—his marketing jobs that he'd walked away from, but she'd already shared too much with him and those confidences felt like vines, wrapping around her. Learning more about this man who already intrigued her so much would only make them bind tighter.

She stood and began cleaning up. Silently, he rose to help, loading her refrigerator with the beer he'd brought, but hadn't drank, and the last few pieces of pizza. They'd be good for lunch tomorrow. Maybe even breakfast.

She was rinsing her wine glass in the sink when he came up behind her. "So what happens now, Kari with a K? You going to spend the next couple of months pretending I don't exist?"

"That would be easiest."

"Would it?"

She shrugged, keeping her back turned. Afraid of what she might see in his eyes if she faced him. Afraid of what he might see in hers. It wasn't her way to ignore an issue, and running from this man had only twisted her up inside. Doing it again made even less sense.

"What do you have in mind, Ty the History Teacher?" she asked softly.

She couldn't see him smile, not when he stood behind her. But she felt it, right down to her toes.

"Cards on the table?" he said in a low voice. "I like you. You're a breath of fresh air. I want to spend some time with you before you move on to that big future of yours. I'm not looking for a woman to make me dinner and babies, Kari. Hell, I wasn't looking at all."

"Yeah, I got that when you waited five days to even see if I was still alive."

It was a tactical error, one that he obviously picked up on right away. He swung around and leaned against the counter beside her so he could see her face . . . so she could see his. A slow smile—the same one that had shimmied her right off her barstool the night she'd met him—spread across his face.

"Have you been waiting for me?" he asked.

"No."

"Counting the hours since the last time we kissed?" he teased.

Hours, minutes . . . he had no idea.

"No," she whispered again.

One small step, that's all he needed to take, but instead, he leaned in, so close she could feel his heat. Still not touching, though. Damn him.

"Liar," he whispered, his breath warm against her ear.

And she wanted more. A lot more. She wanted him to pull her to him. Take her right there on the Formica table.

He straightened and reached for his jacket. "I should be going."

"You should?"

"I've said my piece. Ball's in your court, now."

He shrugged into his coat, leaned down and gave her a soft, slow kiss.

"Drive careful going home."

"But . . . wait. What ball? I don't even have your number."

"Sweetheart, you've had it since hello."

Wasn't that a line from a movie? Her face was hot and a panicky feeling started deep in her belly. She liked the ball better in his court.

He said, "You want me, come find me. Doesn't matter when, doesn't where."

"But . . . ."

"You know where I live, you know where I work. It's not that hard to track me down." He paused and held her gaze. "If that's what you want."

And then he was gone. Kari still hadn't moved when she heard the door open and the cowbell gong. In fact, she'd even forgotten to breathe.

CHAPTER SEVEN

THE NEXT MORNING was a blur of last minute details, and Kari didn't have time to even think.

Yet somehow Ty never left her mind. In fact, he plagued her to distraction.

You want me, come find me . . .

At once a challenge and an appeal. She couldn't resist either one.

The Grand Opening of HardWear was scheduled for Friday, the day after tomorrow. Simone had placed sale ads in the local paper—which as near as Kari could tell was more like a flyer. They'd put signs all around town and sent announcement postcards to a purchased mail list of all residents within a hundred miles of Starlight Bend. The company website was updated, press releases completed, though to date, the media hadn't really cared about anything they did. In short, they were as ready as they'd ever be.

"I don't know about you," Simone said, "But I'm going to drive into Kalispell, check into the most expensive hotel I can find and order some food and a bottle of wine from room service. I'm spending the whole day at the spa tomorrow. Want to join me?"

Kari shook her head. "I don't think so. I want to explore Starlight Bend a bit. I haven't seen many of the sights since I've been here."

"You've seen the bar, you've seen the lake. There's not much more to it."

"You know that's not true. Every one of these towns we've been to has had something cool to see. Who knows, I might even go for a hike tomorrow."

"How are we friends?" Simone asked with a shudder as she pulled on her very expensive cashmere coat.

Simone came from money. The launch of their company was an experiment for her, not her livelihood. For Kari, the scenario was quite a bit different. This chain of stores would be the bedrock of her career . . . or the gravestone, depending on the outcome.

"Have fun at the spa," she said.

"Don't fall off a mountain," Simone answered.

Mountains were the least of her concerns. And of course, the only sights she was interested in could be found on tall, dark and handsome Ty Timberlake. He'd said the ball was in her court and it had been bouncing around inside her, causing all manner of mayhem.

Now, she was in the exact situation she'd tried so hard to avoid. Entangled. With a man she already liked way too much. But winter was in the air and there was something magical about this little town of Starlight Bend. Twice today, she caught herself singing Christmas carols. The holidays were almost here and wouldn't it be nice, for the first time since her parents had died, to spend them with someone special?

Ty was a temptation she couldn't resist—didn't want to resist. That didn't mean her long term plans had to change. It only meant that while she was here, she might try her hand at living a little. What harm could come from that?

She shut down the voice in her head that was more than willing to itemize the harm: broken hearts; broken condoms; broken marriage proposals; death.

Nope, none of that was happening here. Just a little fun, with one of most confident, handsome men she'd ever met.

The ball's in your court.

Indeed, it was. But how would she play it?

She spent extra time on her makeup, striving to achieve that perfectly applied natural look they always had in the commercials. After trying on everything in her closet, she settled on a red sweater dress that fit right in all the right places. Black tights, ankle boots that made her legs look long and shapely, and a chunky, silver necklace and matching earrings finished the outfit off.

Nervous as hell, she stepped outside into the bracing cold. A low November sky promised more snow was coming, and likely soon. For some reason, that put a bounce in her step. She even caught herself humming *Baby It's Cold Outside.*

He'd said come find him. She'd considered waiting at his house, but that felt too stalker-ly, skulking at the curb until he showed up. So she'd chosen work. He'd come to her place of business, so it felt like fair play.

Starlight Bend High School shared grounds with the Junior High and Elementary schools. The three building were situated at the edge of town, mountains at their back, open fields all around. A forlorn playground shivered in the brisk wind.

By the time she stepped out of her car, a stampeding heard of butterflies had settled in her stomach and she felt flushed from face to feet, but she squared her shoulders and went inside, feeling like she was stepping back in time. Trophy cases and banners decorated the main hallway of the high school, including one that invited them all to the winter dance, just four weeks away. The hall smelled faintly of french fries and vegetable soup and brought a rush of her own memories to the surface.

She'd been an awkward adolescent who hadn't grown into her feet—literally—until after college, and even then she couldn't stop tripping over them. That was then, though. Now, she was the woman in the red dress who'd come to claim her sexy history teacher. A full orchestra should be playing a background overture as she sashayed down the hall.

The office was to the right, where a young woman sat behind a high counter, reviewing what appeared to be attendance sheets. Turkey and pilgrim decorations were taped to the walls, but a collection of elves circled her computer, poised to herald Christmas. She looked up when Kari walked in. Around the same age as Kari, she had black hair, bright blue eyes and a quick smile.

65

She looked vaguely familiar, but it wasn't until Kari read her name from the plastic badge pinned to her sweater, that it clicked. Marianne. The one who'd annoyed Stan, the grouchy bartender, with Christmas songs the night Kari had met Ty.

"I know who you are," Marianne said with a big grin.

That could mean a lot of things, and Kari felt a rush of heat at her hairline. Ty had warned her that everyone in town would know she'd gone home with him, but she hadn't expected anyone to shout it out. A woman sitting at a desk next to the principal's office looked up.

"You're opening that new store, aren't you?" Marianne went on.

The store. Not the monkey sex. Relieved, Kari said, "That's right."

"Well, good luck with that. The men in this town don't know a thing about dressing. Wrangler jeans and worn out boots. That's all I ever see. Half the time, my fiancé—" she held up her hand so Kari could admire her ring—"looks like he just climbed off a horse when he picks me up."

"Send him to the store, then. We'll dress him up."

"*Phht*," she said. "He won't go. He's not the kind of guy who's ever going to fuss over how he looks. That's how the men around here are."

It was how they were in every other town, too. With the first couple of stores, the challenge of changing their minds had kept her going. But the battle never ended, and the fight had lost its appeal. She was ready for something new.

"You're here to see Mr. T, aren't you?" Marianne said with a knowing look. "He said you might be stopping by to meet his class."

"He did?"

She didn't know whether to be pissed off at his arrogance or grateful that he'd paved the way.

"Uh-huh," Marianne said, opening a desk drawer and pulling out a stack of name tags. "You have to wear one of these at all times and I'll have to escort you."

"Okay." Kari wrote her name on the tag and stuck it to her chest.

"All right then. Welcome to SBHS, Kari."

Marianne chattered as she came around and out of the swinging half-door, telling Kari more than she ever wanted to know about life as a high school secretary. She was a tall woman, with big bones and a long stride. Kari had on high heels and barely reached her shoulder. If Ty's class had been far, she'd have been out of breath when they got there. Fortunately, it was a straight shot down the main hall, past rows of lockers and closed doors.

Marianne stopped in front of one on the right. Kari could hear Ty's deep voice coming from inside. Carefully, she peeked through the window.

He stood in front of the class, wearing a chunky cream sweater, faded jeans, and cowboy boots. And he wore them damn well. His dark hair looked unruly and his light eyes, electric as he lectured. For the most part, he was holding the attention of the twenty or so students, but one boy noticed her peering in.

She stepped back before he spoke up.

"And what happened in July of 1806?" Ty asked, his voice drifting out. Silence met his question. "Come on people. July, 1806?"

"Lewis and Clarke," a female voice answered.

"Lewis and Clarke!" Ty agreed enthusiastically. "That's right. The Louisiana purchase enabled Lewis and Clarke to—"

"Mr. T?" a male voice interrupted.

"What, Josh?"

"There's a girl outside your door."

Ty turned his head and his eyes met Kari's through the safety glass and Kari's lungs forgot how to work. She was pretty sure her heart had stuttered to a stop as well. Her fingers tingled when she opened the door. Ty hadn't moved.

"Miss Dale," he said in that deep voice, the one that was heard by other parts of her body, not just her ears.

And all of her carefully planned words went right out of her head. She'd had a witty line about a ball, her court, returning it, but she couldn't remember it now and she felt like an idiot, standing in his doorway with nothing to say.

"Go on," Marianne whispered encouragingly.

"I, um, tracked you down," she mumbled.

Which was so not the sparkling line she'd played in her mind. But Ty hit her with a smile that made her knees feel weak and suddenly words didn't matter.

"Get your books out," Ty said, not looking at his

68

rapt class. "Page 113. I'll be back in five minutes and each of you better have one fact to share about Lewis and Clarke."

"Is that your girlfriend, Mr. T?" one of the boys asked as Ty caught Kari's hand and led her out the door.

Marianne was still standing in the hall and Ty faltered, surprised to see her. "Escort," Marianne explained. "I can watch your class for a minute, if you need me to."

"That would make you my new best friend," he answered.

Marianne laughed and went to babysit his class. Ty took Kari's hand and led her down the hall to a door without a window and pulled her inside. Desks and music stands were stacked around the walls, along with a podium, a piano, and a stand of flags.

He closed the door and pressed her up against it. "I was hoping you weren't going to wait five days before you showed up."

"I thought about it," she said. "But I just couldn't see the point."

His mouth covered hers, his lips warm, his kiss hungry. His hands moved from her cheeks, to her shoulders, down the arch of her back, to her hips. Kari melted into him, letting him mold her body to his. Wondering how she'd stayed away from him for so long. He made her moan; he made her rock her hips into his. He made her lose her mind and not even care.

He tasted fresh, minty, and darkly sexual. She wanted to strip him right there in the storage room. Her hands were already beneath his sweater. He'd been working on her senses since the moment he'd packed up his satchel and moved down the bar to sit with her. Like a drug, once sampled, forever craved.

Too soon he lifted his mouth from hers, but he didn't move away. Not that she'd have let him if he'd tried. With a soft smile, the kind that was just for her, he rested his forehead against hers.

"I have to get back to my class."

"I know. But I was wondering—"

"Yes," he said.

"You don't know what I'm going to ask."

"Doesn't matter. The answer's yes." He cupped her face and kissed her again. "Yes."

"How long until you're finished here?"

"Not until six. Hockey practice. I'm one of the coaches."

"Of course you are," she said and caught his bottom lip with hers. "Come over when you're done. My place is out on McK—"

"I know where you live," he said, his breath hot on her skin.

"Bring your pajamas," she whispered back. "Or not."

"Yes," he muttered, pushing his leg between hers, his thigh tight against the sweet spot at the apex of her legs. He kissed her like he might never stop. That was okay with Kari.

At last, he lifted his head and reluctantly stepped back. Kari sighed with disappointment and pulled her hands from under his sweater. He held the door for her and followed into the hallway.

"Bring Buttercup, too," she said in a low voice before they reached his room. "You're not going to be home tonight."

She looked over her shoulder as she walked away. Ty had stopped in front of his door to watch her. She could feel his heated gaze long after she stepped outside.

CHAPTER NINE

IF SHE WENT home now, she'd drive herself crazy waiting for Ty to get there. She decided it would be a good time to do some exploring and check out the only real competition HardWear had in a hundred-mile radius. The store called Big Sky Living was just past the edge of town. It carried sporting goods and outdoor wear and serviced several communities. By all accounts, it did a respectable business.

Big Sky Living was huge, but then again, so was everything she'd encountered in Montana, from sky to personalities. It had a sprawling, open floor plan and racks of clothing and gear. Not surprisingly, camouflage seemed to be the color of the season. Relieved that the overlap in their stock seemed minimal, Kari wandered to the enormous Christmas tree in the center of the store.

"Impressive, isn't it?" a deep voice asked from beside her.

Surprised, Kari turned to find an older, weathered version of the man she couldn't get out of her thoughts standing there. He wore a cowboy hat, sheepskin jacket, jeans and boots. He should have had a horse tied to a nearby hitching post—which they still had in Starlight Bend, by the way. There was no doubt that this was Ty's father. The resemblance was too strong for him not to be.

"You're one of the ladies who bought my store, aren't you?"

"If you're Henry Timberlake, I am." She held out her hand. "Kari Dale."

He shook it. "Pleasure to meet you, Kari."

"Likewise."

She smiled and went back to admiring the grand Christmas tree. "How in the hell did they get it through the door?" she asked.

Henry laughed, sounding so much like his son that it startled her. She'd expected him to be a hunched and bitter man, not just like his son.

"They built the store around it," he said. "A wonder, isn't it?"

Hell, yes, it was.

Santa and his helpers were already in residence, and a crowd of bright-eyed children had gathered around.

"Shouldn't they be in school?" she asked.

"Field trips. They come each year from all around—kids that wouldn't have anything otherwise. This is Starlight Bend's Wish Tree and they're here to hang their Christmas wishes on the branches. The rest of us get to be Santa Claus to them."

"Nice," she said softly. "I like that."

"They light the tree up right after Halloween, so we all have time to get our shopping done."

"Is that why you're here?"

He nodded. "It's my favorite time of year."

"Can anyone . . . ." she nodded at the tree.

"Grant a wish? You bet. Come on."

He led the way, grinning over his shoulder. Decorated cards and snowflakes hung on nearly every branch of the tree, interspersed with an occasional nondescript envelope or folded piece of paper.

Henry saw her looking. "Those usually come from the older children," he said. "They don't decorate their wishes, but they make them all the same."

She nodded, remembering those rough years after her parents died when she'd worked two jobs while going to school just to make ends meet. A Wish Tree would have come in handy back then. Henry circled the tree a few times before he finally selected a glittery paper ornament from one of the branches.

"What's your criteria?" Kari asked, amused at how much time he put into the decision.

"One calls to me," he said solemnly. "Happens every year. Sometimes I do three or four of them, but one at a time. That's why I start so early. Brings me joy."

She nodded, charmed by his delight and sincerity. Henry followed her as she strolled around the tree, closing her eyes and breathing in the scent of pine. It had been such a long time since she'd thought of Christmas as more than a retail blitz. Now, a feeling of peace filled her. This Christmas she might have someone to share it with. The idea excited and terrified her.

She opened her eyes and found that one of the big-kid envelopes was right in front of her. Deciding that was as much of a call as she was likely to get, Kari took it down.

"That the one?" Henry asked.

"I guess so."

He nodded, a knowing smile on his face. "You don't think it called to you, do you?"

"Not really. But that's okay. I'll enjoy buying the gifts."

"It's not about that, though. You may not even figure it out until later, but if you picked that wish, it was meant for you. Open it up."

He watched with bright eyes as she unfolded the paper inside. The page was a copied fill-in-the-blank form with pre-filled information up top: first name, age, and sizes for shirts, pants, coats and shoes. Below was space for the wishers to elaborate on their wishes. This one was from Sara, a fourteen-year-old girl of average size who had round, awkward penmanship and to-the-point requests.

"*Dear Santa,*" Kari read aloud. "*I don't want anything for myself and that's not because I'm such a nice person, either. What I want is for my mom to stay clean when she gets out of rehab. I want her to take care of us. And I want to quit being weird and fit in. But I know you don't have any of those things in your red bag, so why bother asking? What's important right now are my little brother and sister. For Max, please bring one of those big furry toys from the Star Wars movie. They're called Wookies. He has a miniature one and he's played with it so much he's worn off the face. Max thinks he's part Wookie. I'm pretty sure he's right. For my sister Alyssa, please bring a Loopdedoo Kit. I hope you know what that is, because I don't. She says she can make bracelets and jewelry with it. Thank you. Sincerely, Sara Carson."*

Kari stared at the signature and something inside her softened.

"See," Henry said gently.

"I can remember making that same wish," she said. "To be normal, just like everyone else. I guess it's not until we grow up that we figure out no one is normal. And if they were, they'd be boring."

Henry nodded. "You got a good one."

"What about you?"

"This kid wants a horse, but he'll settle for a car so his dad can get to work. If that's not possible, socks will do, because his feet get cold at night."

Kari blinked at the sudden moisture in her eyes. "He doesn't want much, does he?"

"Those are the best ones."

She nodded silently and looked up at the tree again, thinking of her own childhood wishes. Her parents had done their best, but there'd never been enough money. Ever.

"Family's a funny thing, isn't it?"

"Funny," Henry agreed.

"What you'll do for it, what they'll do for you. And

then, sometimes, it just cuts you right open," she said softly. "Like a knife."

Ty's father was silent a moment then said, "They sure do."

"Sometimes you have to just get away."

"Well, that's a knife, too, isn't it?"

The sharpness in his tone made her look at him, recalling what little Ty had told her about their relationship.

"How so?" she asked carefully. This was new territory, asking someone she hardly knew about their life. Funny coincidence that it should be with another Timberlake.

"Family should stay in the family," Henry said sharply. "Family shouldn't up and leave and go do whatever the hell they want, whenever they want."

In her gut, she knew they were talking about Ty and the work-in-progress relationship that existed between father and son. Ty had been hired right out of college and gone to Detroit. Was his leaving the bone of contention between them?

"People have dreams," she said warily. "Family should understand that, right?"

Eyes narrowed now, Henry looked away. "Maybe they should. Maybe they shouldn't."

"But what's the alternative?" she said. "I mean, estrangement? Anger? For how long? Just because someone followed their dream?"

"Dreams have been known to hurt people," the old man said grimly.

"Only if someone uses them as a weapon," she retorted sharply.

He looked stunned. In truth, she'd shocked herself. She wasn't usually a meddler, but in Henry's bluster, she saw pain. Real pain. She'd seen it in Ty's eyes, too.

"I'm sorry," she said swiftly, backing away from the genuine human connection that had sprung up beneath the evergreen Wish Tree and, true to form, turned messy. "I don't know what I'm saying. It's none of my business."

"No, it's not. But I get the feeling that doesn't stop you much."

"I think it's the air here," she muttered. "It's messed with my filter."

Henry stared at her for a minute and then smiled. "It's okay. A good woman needs a little unfiltered sass."

Before she could think of a response, the Santa she'd seen earlier appeared beside them and raised a hand, *ho-ho-ho-ing* at them. Close up, she was amazed at the detail in his costume. The white hair and beard looked real and the blue eyes sparkled merrily. The suit had a soft, worn look to it—not felt, but velvet.

He shook a small red bag, then held it out to her. "Go on," he said when she hesitated. "Pick one."

Smiling, Kari reached in and pulled out a small white card. One side was blank, but the other had, *Your wish has been granted,* printed with a careful hand in glittery green ink.

Kari looked up. "I didn't make a wish."

Santa didn't say anything, but those twinkling eyes laughed at her. He shook the bag again and held it out for Henry.

Henry squinted back at Santa. "Who are you?" he asked. "What happened to Charlie Connor?"

Santa just smiled and gave another jolly old chuckle. Disgruntled, Henry turned away without taking a card from Santa's bag. A moment later, she saw him talking to someone who worked there. Kari wandered around a bit before he caught up with her again at the front of the store.

"The manager says Charlie moved away," he said sadly. "Didn't even say goodbye."

"Were you good friends?"

"Nah. Just here. But I wish sometimes that I could nail people's feet down. You know? Keep them from leaving."

Like his wife, who was now married to a ukulele player. Like Ty, who'd needed to strike out on his own, if only for a little while.

"You're never going to win that battle, Henry."

"No, I don't suppose I will. Can't fault me for trying, though." He took a deep breath. "You have yourself a good day, Kari."

"You, too, Henry," she said, watching him walk out the door as *Silver Bells* played over the store's speakers.

CHAPTER TEN

THE STARLIGHT BEND High School Hockey Team had had a stellar season and now they were moving into playoffs, which meant they had to practice. But that didn't mean Ty had to like it. His thoughts weren't on ice, pucks, or plays. They were centered on a beautiful woman with September eyes and the lips of an angel.

He worked the team hard, but ended practice twenty minutes early. In record time, he swung home, showered, grabbed Buttercup and all her doggy stuff, then he was off, only stopping to pick up some wine and a bouquet of flowers from the stand at the front of the market.

He was nervous, he realized. He hadn't been this revved up over a woman in . . . ever. And Kari wasn't just any woman. That first night, he'd known she'd be hard to keep, but at the time, he hadn't known how much he'd want to keep her. Now, the thought that circled in his head was simply, how? How did a man hold onto the likes Kari Dale?

He didn't have the answer. Yet. He refused to believe that one didn't exist, though. And his own determined fixation rattled him. She'd worked her way beneath his skin and she hadn't even been trying. In fact, the opposite was true. If he'd left it up to her, she'd have stuck to her plans and never looked back.

Except . . . and this was the part that had him churned up inside . . . when given the choice, when told the ball was in her court, she'd come to him. He smiled, remembering that powerful feeling that had gripped him when he saw her standing outside his door.

Jesus, he was a mess. He sounded like one of his students, instead of a grown man who'd been out in the world, who'd made his own way. But things had always come easy to Ty. Money, success, recognition . . . women.

Until Kari Dale, the girl who never truly unpacked her bags.

"What do you think, Buttercup?"

Buttercup sat in the passenger seat beside him, tongue lolling, eyes adoring when she looked his way.

Kari opened her door when he pulled up, looking like something he must have dreamed. She was too beautiful to be real, all gorgeous hair and hazel eyes. Flowers in one hand, everything else in the other, Ty made his way up the snow covered walk with Buttercup on his heels. Kari smiled boldly and stepped back for them to enter, kneeling down to stroke the little dog.

She'd changed into a soft jersey that clung to her breasts and fell to her thighs. Leggings covered her shapely legs and fluffy pink slippers were on her feet. She couldn't have been sexier if she'd been wearing fishnets and high heels.

"Hi," he said.

She looked up. "Hi."

They stared at one another for a moment, grinning like idiots, the tight rope of excitement binding them both. This was a *moment*, the kind that became a memory. The kind that marked a new direction in the journey.

She'd come to him. He understood how monumental that was for this woman. And he wanted to make sure she understood it, too. The game had changed, now. And they both had skin in it.

She stood slowly, hands nervous at her sides. Ty remembered the flowers and held them out. Her gaze went all soft and dewy. "Flowers," she murmured, burying her face in the bouquet. "Thank you."

Deep inside, something turned.

"Are you hungry?" she asked, breathless. "I made dinner."

"Should I take that as a sign you don't like me anymore?"

"No," she said softly, blushing.

She took his hand and led him into the kitchen where a host of good smells waited. She'd cooked—*for him*—and he was hungry. He hadn't eaten since lunch and his belly felt hollow. But another hunger trumped his growling stomach. A hunger of the mind and body for this woman.

He tucked Buttercup's bed under the table where she'd like it, and set the food and dish on top of the counter. "Get on your bed, girl," he told the little dog.

Wagging her tail happily, she did as she was told.

Kari's calendar caught his eye when he turned. It displayed three months at a time. October had a big *X* through it, but each day in November had its own mark. A countdown, complete with numbers in the corners. Nothing like a little reality to dampen the mood.

They didn't have time to waste.

He caught her in his arms when she turned from the vase she'd put the flowers in and kissed her hard. She'd been waiting, at least that's how it felt as she surged into his arms, warm and soft and sweetly scented. After she'd left the school today, he'd had to sit behind his desk for the rest of his class to hide his hard on. Even the next class, because his erection never really went away. And now she was in his arms, her mouth hot against his and her hands all over him. He hadn't intended to come through the door like a cave man, but he couldn't let her go. Not now.

"Do you need to turn the oven off," he asked, his mouth on her throat. "I don't think we're going to be eating for a while."

"Crockpot," she answered, titling her head to the side so he had full access. "It's fine."

The house was small, the bedroom not hard to find. But the floor would have worked, too. That's how much he needed her. He didn't rush, though. Couldn't, when his fingers wanted to linger over every inch they touched. Her hair was so soft and it smelled like flowers. The skin at her throat was fragrant, too. Silky and pale, warm beneath his lips.

She moved with him, her body restless, as needy as his, her hands exploring, lingering. He pushed the stretchy material of her leggings down and slid his hand between her thighs. She was so hot, so ready. She moaned and bucked and Ty nearly came undone.

He had to let her go, but just long enough to strip her clothes. The jersey came off, revealing bare breasts and warm skin. He tugged her leggings the rest of the way down, skimming panties along with them. She kicked them off the rest of the way. On his knees in front of her, Ty groaned. She was perfect and she fit him like she'd been made for it.

He pressed his open mouth to the tender spot between belly and pubic bone, breathing in the sultry scent of her. They worked together on his clothes, until they were both stripped bare.

"I can't keep my hands off you," he muttered, finding the curve of her buttocks, the hollows of her throat, the soft weight of her breasts, the ripple of ribs. She stroked him freely from breastbone to belly, her touch, warm and light until she circled him with her fingers and the touch became seductive . . . possessive. He wasn't alone in this cyclone of need.

He couldn't wait any longer, not if he wanted to stay sane. With a groan, he pushed her back against the pillows and found a place between her spread thighs to settle, to begin. He was so aroused that even the light sheath of the condom caused pain, the good kind. The kind he wanted more of.

And then, at last, he was inside her. Deep within

that hot fist of her body. She arched, making a sound that he remembered. It danced over his senses and drove him to a place beyond the physical. He could spend his whole life trying to illicit that sound and never grow tired of it.

Kari matched his rhythm, bowing her body to meet his, bracing her feet to lift her hips. He palmed her mons, letting his thumb slide down and toy with the tight point of nerves at the top, feeling her gasp and pant as he brought her closer and closer. She moaned his name as she came, her brows pulled together, her teeth sunk into her bottom lip.

His orgasm lacked the elegance of hers, but it came from some unfathomable place inside him, ripping through his body in a burst of agonizing pleasure. He feared he was crushing her, but she'd wrapped her arms and legs around him so tightly that they became one continuous vibration. She came again with him buried so deeply in her body that he felt the muscles gripping, refusing to let go even as her breath came hot against his throat and her heart pounded in tandem with his.

She didn't let him catch his breath. With a twist and a push of her leg, she rolled them both until she was seated on his hips, still connected by the pulsing of their sex. Slowly, sinuously, she began to move, lifting so slightly, reseating herself more completely. He was rock hard in an instant, ready to claim her again. Make her his for now, for always. But even as he captured her mouth in a slow, endless kiss, even as his body thrust into hers, bringing them both to that point of no return, the question emerged.

How could he make Kari Dale stay?

CHAPTER ELEVEN

THEY HAD DINNER in bed, naked, laughing at the slippery spaghetti noodles, sharing a fork, a bowl. Touching Ty, being with him like this . . . she was drunk from the way he made her feel.

She trailed her fingers over his strong arms and broad chest, the ridges of rib and abdomen, loving the way sinew and bone shaped him, the feel of the masculine terrain that was so different from her own soft curves. Each time she turned to him, Ty seemed to feel the same way and he never tired of bringing them both to that dizzy, crazy place of climax.

At last they'd moved to the living room, but they hadn't bothered with clothes. Ty started a fire and Kari pulled the quilt off the bed so they could wrap themselves together beneath it. Shyly, Buttercup left her bed and curled in the trailing ends of the blanket. Kari leaned down to scratch behind her ear before snuggling up to Ty again.

"I met your dad today," Kari said after a while, her head resting on his chest. She turned her face so she could see his expression.

"Where?" he asked, head back. Giving nothing

away

"The big Christmas tree at that store outside of town."

"The Wishing Tree," he said with a small nod. "He loves granting wishes. When I was a kid, I used to think it was a magic tree. I was jealous of the kids who got to use it."

"I thought all the gifts went to underprivileged children?"

"They do. I didn't really know what that meant at the time, though."

She smiled against his skin. "What would you have wished for?"

His chest rose with a deep breath and she ran her fingers up from his belly to lay over his heart. "I wanted peace. A happy family. The kind on TV that ate meals together. Made up after they fought. Cared. And didn't try to hurt each other all the time."

She stilled, surprised. "Was it . . . abusive in your house?"

"Nah, not that. There was just always so much *conflict*. No one could get along for more than five minutes—even that was rare. My mom was always mad at my dad or fighting with my grandpa. And Grandpa, he lived to stir the pot. He was a hard man and he was on my dad's back every single day. Nothing he did was ever good enough."

Ty ran his fingertips over her shoulder in an idle caress, but his voice had grown soft, distant. She moved closer, sensing that removing himself emotionally was how he'd coped with the drama of his childhood. Wanting him to stay connected with her.

"What happened between you and your dad?" she asked.

He let out a deep breath. "Sometimes, I don't even know myself. I mean, we always had our issues, but . . . my grandpa never quit being the head of the household, even when the household didn't belong to him. He thought he should—and could—dictate how things should be. He didn't understand the meaning of boundaries, so he'd jump in when my parents were fighting. He'd overrule them when it came to me. Drove my mom batshit."

"Your dad never told him to butt out?"

"It went against the grain, talking back to his father. And Grandpa kept it that way, always cutting the legs out from underneath my dad. Making him feel like he wasn't man enough to manage his life on his own, let alone handle a wife and son."

"That's unconscionable," she said, "his own father undermining him like that."

Ty nodded. "When I got old enough to stand up to my grandpa, I got in the middle of it all. I ended up getting the belt from my dad and my ass chewed from my Gramps. I learned my lesson. No good deed goes unpunished, you know?"

"Is your grandfather still alive?"

"No. He died a week before I left for college."

"That must have been hard on you," she said carefully, knowing that when grief, confusion, anger, and change collided, they could rip a person apart.

"My dad never said it, but it always felt like he blamed me for it. I guess that was easier than accepting that my grandpa's time was up."

She understood that, in a way. She'd lost both of her parents to a car accident when she was eighteen. Her dad had been driving, probably thinking about one of his inventions and not paying attention to the road. He'd over compensated when he'd drifted into oncoming traffic and lost control of the vehicle. It had been sudden, violent, and irrevocable. She'd needed someone else to blame for the devastating loss, but there hadn't been anyone. For a long time, she'd blamed herself, though she hadn't even been with them.

"About a month later," Ty went on, "my mom announced that she was done with Montana and done with my dad. She filed for a divorce, packed her bags, and moved to Hawaii."

"Wow," Kari said, thinking of the pain she'd heard in Henry's voice when they'd spoken. "He must have felt like the whole world had abandoned him."

"Bingo."

Kari propped herself up so she could see his face. He wore an aloof expression—like that would convince them both that he didn't really care what had happened in the past.

"And now that you're back, he won't let you in," she said.

He nodded.

"You think he's afraid you'll hurt him again?"

Ty met her eyes, surprise in the depths of his. "Is that what you think?"

"What else would it be?"

"I guess I thought . . . he and my grandpa loved the store so much. My dad didn't know jack about running it, but he loved it. I had no interest in following in their footsteps, though. I always thought that was what made him so angry. Him selling it to you—kind of proved that."

His eyes were hard, his brow furrowed, the line of muscles in his neck taut.

"You two have a complicated relationship," she said softly.

"I guess that's better than none at all," he muttered.

She climbed in his lap, straddling his thighs so she faced him. "You need to fix things with him, Ty. For the both of you."

He let out a soft laugh and shook his head. "I know. Just haven't figured out how to get there from here."

His hands skimmed up her thighs to her hips. She leaned down and kissed him. "You'll figure it out."

From what she'd seen in Ty, and heard in both his and his father's voices, she believed the two men cared about one another, and they were just too stubborn to admit it.

Men.

He kissed her back. Slow, lingering, and full of all the emotions she could feel inside of him. When she pulled away, his expression was serious. Finally, he gave her a small smile. "Where have you been all my life, Kari with a K?"

"I don't know," she said softly. "I've been on the go since I was eighteen."

That darkened his eyes and banished the smile. She wished she'd kept her big mouth shut.

"Always in such a hurry to be gone, aren't you?" he said softly.

"Maybe not so much in this very minute."

"That's right. I've got you now."

He caught her lips in a kiss that silenced them both and before long, he'd chased away even the thought of leaving. For now.

CHAPTER TWELVE

THE WEEKS FLEW by. During the days, Kari was busy at the store. Customers had come when the doors opened—Ty had been their first and he'd let her outfit him from head to toe. He'd looked damn good, too. But in general, business was sluggish and their revenue alarmingly low. So far, this store had the poorest Grand Opening of any of the other four. If not for the nights she spent with Ty, Kari might have worried herself into an early grave.

But when he had her in his arms, Ty refused to let her stay in her head and obsess over the dollar signs. Not that she had much of choice, once he started touching her. She'd expected her attraction to him to wane over time. She couldn't have been more wrong. He seemed to feel the same—hopelessly addicted to her touch, the feel of her body next to his. Some dark, self-destructive part of her began to think he might be happy about her failure. He'd made it clear that he wanted to her to stay here. With him.

As each day passed, the idea of staying grew in appeal until Kari wasn't certain why she was fighting it. But Ty could never understand what drove her to achieve. He hadn't seen the way failure had broken her father down, had turned her mother into a shrew, had embarrassed Kari until she'd quit bringing her friends home. Quit telling them that her father invented things. In the end, she'd been ashamed of him. Worse, he'd known it.

Failing at this—a different kind of invention—it just couldn't happen. Not to her.

She was surprised, therefore, when Ty walked in the Monday before Thanksgiving and said, "Got a minute?"

"Sure," she answered. She had plenty of minutes, maybe hours before the next customer came in.

He was dressed in the jeans and button down she'd picked out for him and she couldn't help the rush of possessive pride she felt when she saw just how good he looked in them.

"I have an idea that I think will help you," Ty said.

"Help me what?" she asked.

"Generate some revenue, for one. The hockey team has their last game of the season tomorrow night. It's a home game, so they have to wear their best to school tomorrow."

She had a vague memory of high school sports and seeing all the jocks show up in ties on game day.

"How is that a revenue generating idea?" she asked, frowning.

"Instead of wasting any more money on a marketing plan that clearly isn't working, why don't you try living ads?"

Miffed at how blunt he was, she said, "Human

words, please."

"I've been wearing your clothes to school every day. And I know I look good."

Said with an earnest expression, completely lacking in ego. The credit was all hers, that look said. She felt unreasonably sappy as she stared at him, wanting to hug him, maybe even cry a little.

"But I'm an old guy to your demographic. They can think I look good all they want, but they won't be able to picture it for themselves unless they see it on themselves. Why not dress up my hockey team—the *gods* of Starlight Bend High—and let them do the marketing for you."

She blinked at him for a moment while the image formed in her head, twenty-two sturdy young men played for Ty. He told her as much before. They came from different families, different parts of town. They were a diverse pool, products of the American melting pot. And dressed in the HardWear brand of clothes, they would look stunning.

It was a good idea. It was a *great* idea, actually.

"Simone," she called, never looking away from Ty's face. His eyes had a sparkle of excitement and his smile . . . it was just for her.

Simone emerged from the backroom with a napkin in one hand and a bite of her sandwich in the other. Kari turned to Ty. "Tell her what you just said."

Simone wore the same stunned expression as Kari by the time Ty finished. It was such a simple, elegant plan. And she absolutely believed it would have impact.

"They'd be wearing them tomorrow?"

"If I tell them they have the choice of wearing their father's hand-me-down ties or coming here for some free clothes, they'll take the clothes. And they'll wear them."

Simone looked at Kari. "What do you say?"

"What we're doing isn't working. This is the best idea I've heard in a long time."

"Okay then. Let's do it."

Kari grinned at Ty and nodded. "Send them over, Mr. T."

"They'll be here before you close."

Simone thanked him and went back to her lunch. Kari wrapped her arms around him and thanked him quite a bit more.

"My pleasure," Ty said. "Those wheels grinding in your head have been keeping me awake at night."

"Sorry about that."

He shook his head. "No need. I know how important it is for you to succeed here. Get your ticket punched."

Move on . . .

Away from him.

"Doesn't that go against the grain?" she asked, her voice low and serious. "Helping me when you know what it will lead to?"

He cupped her face and kissed the tip of her nose. "Sweetheart, what happens here, to your business? That's not going to be the reason you go or stay. Don't tell me you think it is."

95

She stared into his eyes. She wanted to tell him he was wrong—that her business was the dime that everything turned on. Maybe it had been when she first arrived, but since she'd met Ty, things had changed. *She'd* changed. Every other town, every other venture, she'd only seen as a means to an end. A jumping off point to the next Big Idea in the next town. Settling anywhere had felt like going backwards—something she couldn't do. But her emotions had been at odds with her ambition for weeks now. A lot of it was Ty and how important he'd become to her. But part of it went deeper. Starlight Bend was filled with community—something she'd never had in her life. It had skewed her perspective on how this life of hers should be lived. Going so fast that she never stopped to appreciate a dawning day or crisp evening—was that really living? Did it matter what she achieved if she never took the time to enjoy it?

He smiled at her and shook his head. "I don't want you by default, anyway," he said. "Either you choose me, or you don't. I've already made my decisions."

He grabbed her by the shoulders, lifted her off her feet, and planted a kiss on her that made her toes curl with delight. When he set her down again, he said, "Figure things out, Kari. We're running out of time."

CHAPTER THIRTEEN

DRESSING THE HOCKEY team had been a brilliant idea and it worked like a charm. The team even won their home game, and Kari and Simone had been there to watch it. The very next day, business took a turn for the better. Customers were waiting for them to open their doors in the morning, and by the time they closed shop that night, Kari was filled with hope for record sales on Black Friday.

The week before, Ty had invited her to Thanksgiving dinner at his house. He and a group of friends had been rotating host duties for years. Kari hadn't been to a Thanksgiving dinner since her parents died and was inexplicably nervous about joining people she hardly knew for such an important day. It seemed like a lot of work for little reward and it always made her bittersweet. Too much family time for someone who no longer had any family. But Ty wouldn't take *no* for an answer.

"This is our fourth year and it's my turn to host."

"And you're inviting me because you think I'll help cook?" she asked incredulously.

"Hell, no. I know how to put a turkey in the oven.

Everything else is potluck. You can bring pie. Doesn't even have to be homemade."

"Oh, believe me, it won't be. What about your dad?" she asked. "Do you invite him to join your little celebration?"

"I did. The first year. He told me to stuff my turkey where the sun doesn't shine."

"Ouch."

"I told him the invitation was always open. He told me to put my open invitation in the same place."

"I'm sorry, Ty."

"It's nothing I haven't heard before, sweetheart."

"So if he doesn't spend it with you, who does he spend it with?"

"Last I heard, Becky Smith had taken him under her wing."

Becky from the café? "Lucky Henry. I'll be buying my pies from her, just in case you were wondering."

"I knew I could count on you. Last year one of the teachers brought the pies. She made them herself."

He grimaced and Kari laughed.

"I'm not surprised about Becky, though," she said. "I thought there was a vibe between them the last time I went for my morning coffee."

Ty looked amazed. "What kind of vibe?"

"The kind that gets a guy a seat at Thanksgiving dinner. I'm glad he's not spending it alone."

"Yeah, I'm glad, too."

And in his voice, she heard the other note. The

sadness that he and his father would be at separate tables, in separate houses. Never together.

When she arrived on Thanksgiving Day, Ty opened the front door with an apron around his waist and a smile on his face. He didn't wait to pull her in for a kiss that she felt deep inside.

That morning, she'd marked another day off her calendar, feeling like her departure date had become a predator that stalked her. That threatened to take away the happiness that she'd felt since coming here.

For weeks now, she'd been telling herself that a long distance relationship could work. She'd even convinced herself that she could talk Ty into it, too. Since she'd met him, Ty had somehow managed to steal the core of her, the very heart. If he didn't come with her, would he give it back when she left? Or would she be forever missing that piece of herself? Wasn't that what she'd been afraid of from the start? The reason why she'd bolted the morning after?

"You look like you need some wine," someone said from inside Ty's house.

In moments, she was pulled into their warm and friendly circle. Ty was a laid-back host who had plenty of wine and beer to go with all the food everyone brought. Before long, they progressed from stilted introductions to hilarious stories about growing up in Starlight Bend, getting in trouble in a town where everyone knew your parents. She enjoyed the company and yet, at the same time, she became increasingly aware of how little she had in common with these people. With this town. They had roots sunk so deep, their parents had shared childhood memories. Kari had been transient her entire life, moving from new start to new start with her mom and dad, until they'd hit the dead-end of Dunlap, New Mexico, where they'd left her to survive on her own. She'd never stayed in one place long enough to fit in.

She wouldn't be here long enough, either.

It was with relief that she finally stood to leave. "Tomorrow's Black Friday," she told Ty's friends when they protested. "We open at seven and don't close until ten. It's going to be a long day."

Ty walked her to her car, a cautious light in his eyes. "You don't want to stay tonight?" he asked.

"I do, but I have to be up early and . . . ."

He cocked his head to the side, watching her. She had the feeling that he knew what was going on inside her head.

He pulled her into his arms and kissed her. She met the kiss hungrily, needing him to chase away the shadows inside her. She held him tight and lost herself in all the good that was Ty Timberlake.

When he finally lifted his head, his eyes held a satisfied gleam. "I'll see you tomorrow night, then," he said against her lips.

And even though the voice of sanity told her it was wrong to say yes, to encourage him when there was no future for them, Kari heard herself agree. "See you tomorrow night."

Her house felt empty when she got home. No

surprise, there. That was how she liked things. Quiet, orderly. Temporary. It was easier that way. She could leave when she wanted to without looking back. She had a plan, one she'd honed to perfection. Unlike her father, she would see the fruits of her labor. She would find that shimmery success that had always eluded him. And she would seize it with both hands.

She couldn't do that if she was looking over her shoulder. If she was missing what she'd left behind. Success required clarity and purpose.

Not an aching heart. Not regret.

She stared at the calendar on her wall. Forty more nights. That's all the time she had left here. Mentally, she braced herself and nodded.

Forty nights and she'd be gone.

Chapter Fourteen

The next day was so busy that by the time Kari looked up, it was nearly eleven p.m. She'd missed dinner. She may have missed lunch, too. She couldn't remember. There'd been so many shoppers, so many credit cards handed over from mothers who'd come as far as Billings, Boise, even *Alberta*. Their sons wanted clothes like the Starlight Bend hockey players wore. They'd seen Ty's "living ads" in person or on Snapchat, Instagram, or Facebook. Or they'd simply heard from a friend of a friend. If she could have kissed every boy on the hockey team, she would have.

Ty had called around seven and she'd told him not to count on seeing her that night. He was understanding, and yet there'd been a dark note in his voice when he'd said goodbye. She couldn't help but think that maybe he'd been staring at a calendar, too.

And not in a good way. It was something to think about later, when she had the time.

But *later* seemed to be an elusive horizon that never came. Because the next day was just as busy, a continuous blur of shoppers and Christmas music from the playlist Simone had made. Even after they turned it off, Kari could still hear it in her head. And the day after? Busier still. During a rare lull on Sunday, Simone told her to take five.

"You haven't had a break all day. Go, before they start coming back."

Afraid if she sat down she'd never stand up again, Kari took the break, hoping a caffeine pick-me-up would get her through the rest of the night. She was filling up the coffee pot when she felt him behind her. Big, warm, and smelling so good she almost groaned.

His hands slid up her hips, one slipping down, over her belly to cup her sex, the other moving high to her breast.

"Ty," she breathed. "What are you doing here?"

He pressed his hips into her, letting her feel the hard length of him. Letting her work out what he was doing on her own.

"We can't. Simone might…."

He pressed again, a slow grind that spoke to every neglected nerve in her body. God, she'd missed him. It had only been three days since she'd seem him, but it felt like forever.

Slowly, she turned in his arms, her gaze finding his as he shifted his hands, keeping her in his grasp. He stared down at her with hooded eyes but she saw the fires burning there, the edge of need that was as sharp as a blade.

Silently, he inched the hem of her skirt up her thighs, then slipped his hands under, against her skin. She loved his hands—they were big, like everything about him, and roughened. Man's hands. All over her.

His thumbs hooked in her panties and began working them down. Right there, in the tiny back room kitchen while *Blue Christmas* played in the store.

"Ty—"

"Shhhhh," he said against her lips.

And she shushed. Because now his fingers were inside her and the ability to speak . . . think . . . breathe . . . it was all too difficult. She didn't protest when he lifted her, spun around and set her on the table, just like in her fantasies. Her fingers were there first when he reached for his fly, working the buttons free, finding him ready, satin over steel. The moan in her throat was primal and it sparked an already smoldering fire.

Her head fell back when he finally entered her, hot and hard and demanding. They covered each other's mouths as he drove deeper, pushing her to an edge she needed. Deep, in places that had never held such irresistible cravings. Her muffled cry escaped his fingers. His groan made her come again. She didn't care if Simone walked in on them. She wouldn't have cared if they'd been stripped bare in the middle of Main Street. The power of his touch had become more important than anything else. Her body rejoiced and he rejuvenated her, mind and soul. It shouldn't be possible, the effect he had on her. Yet, denying it was pointless.

Afterwards, he helped her straighten her clothes and stand. Her legs felt wobbly, but everything else felt wonderful. He caught her lips in a long, slow kiss.

"I'll let you get back to work now. Just wanted you

to know I've been missing you."

With a wicked smile, he left her in the tiny backroom kitchen, but it took her a long time before she was ready to get back to work.

CHAPTER FIFTEEN

IN STARLIGHT BEND, Christmas was a state of being. The people who lived here were friendly all the time, but now, with snowflakes falling and chestnuts roasting, carolers dressed in long dresses with fur muffs, the season had taken hold and worked its magic, even on Kari. Every sale was accompanied with a "Merry Christmas," every glance had a smile. The café buzzed with talk of a Winter Carnival and Wish Tree giving. Kari tried not to get too caught up in it, but good cheer was a contagious disease, it seemed.

Still, in quiet moments Kari found herself looking inward and finding only worries.

Out of necessity, she and Simone hired four additional sales clerks and ordered a surplus of stock, because they'd completely sold out of several styles of jeans and at least five of the shirts. And when Kari finally had the chance to check in with their other stores, she learned that sales were up there, too. Significantly, so. The fuse they'd lit five years ago had finally reached the gunpowder. The HardWear brand was about to explode in all the right ways.

It was a dream come true. Everything she'd worked

so hard for was happening now, so fast she could hardly catch her breath. She should be skipping in the streets, belting out Christmas songs with the carolers. Instead, she wanted to slam on the brakes.

She couldn't stop thinking of the giant Wishing Tree and the card she'd pulled from Santa's bag.

Your wish is granted.

So why did she feel like someone had cut all the heads off of her flowers? Why wasn't she ecstatic over the revenue that just kept rising? The realization that, thanks to Ty, the plan she'd crafted was about to succeed?

Her calendar mocked her every day now and each *X* she'd made felt like a wound that would never heal.

Your wish is granted.

She'd already ordered the gifts for the children in the letter she'd pulled from the tree. She'd shopped online and found the Wookie and Loopdedoo Kit— which could, indeed, be used to make bracelets and necklaces. She'd even found something for fourteen-year-old Sara. Something that would make the young woman feel just like everyone else. The outfit Kari had ordered came from Abercrombie Kids—the ultimate equalizer. She'd paired the perfect jeans and the perfect top with the perfect boots. Understated, totally cool. With labels, because girls her age knew their labels. Sara would be dressed like ninety percent of the adolescent girls her age—only she'd be wearing the original brand, not just the knock off.

Still, Kari hated the idea of playing to the social

norms. Of turning spunky Sara of the Wish Tree into a clone. Average. Ordinary. The opposite of weird.

The opposite of special.

Words that sounded like a death sentence for the young woman who'd spoken so bluntly to Santa, placing her brother and sister above her own needs. Refusing to ask for help with something she'd deemed unchangeable.

Kari had wrapped the other two gifts for the younger siblings and had them sitting on the table, ready to deliver. But she just couldn't bring herself to box up the outfit, let alone wrap it in frolicking reindeer paper with a big red bow on top.

Sighing, she left it alone and got ready for her date with Ty. It was Friday night—her first night off since Thanksgiving—and he wanted to take her out. Staying in and having dinner in bed would have suited her just fine, but the truth of the matter was that the harder she worked at distancing her emotions, the more she failed. She couldn't wait to be with him—anywhere. They were both quiet, though, as he drove from her house to the outskirts of town. He'd promised her the best steak of her life and, evidently, The Pinnacle was the place to get it.

The restaurant was lovely, with beautiful views of the mountains, and heavenly smells coming from the kitchen. *Let It Snow* played softly in the bar where they had a drink while waiting for their table. In a room full of revelry and sparkling lights, though, both Kari and Ty remained subdued. For some inexplicable reason, the jolly customers and festive ambiance made her want to cry. Not just a few tears either.

At last a hostess led them to a booth in a secluded, candlelit corner, and Ty slid in beside her. A chill had settled in her bones and she welcomed his heat. Only after the waiter had taken their orders and poured their wine, did either of them speak.

"You're quiet tonight," she observed.

"I was going to say the same to you. Got something on your mind?"

You. Always you.

She took a deep breath and slowly let it out. "I don't know. Maybe. I keep thinking about Sara—the girl whose letter I chose from the Wish Tree."

"Okay," he said with a wary glance.

"Henry—your dad—"

"I do know who he is."

She smiled. "Sorry."

"What about Henry?"

"He said that the card picks you, not the other way around. Do you think that's true?"

"In a way, sure. But it's hard not to feel an affinity for any of the kids that put their wishes on that tree. They're all missing something and that's a feeling we can all relate to one way or another. Right?"

Kari sipped her wine and nodded. Ty had already picked out, purchased, and delivered his Wish Tree gifts earlier in the week. She knew she was making it more difficult than it needed to be.

"So I guess that leads to the bigger the question," he

went on. "What are you missing, Kari?"

She didn't have an answer. Not one she could share, anyway. "It's just . . . there's something about what Sara asked for—what she *didn't* ask for—that hit me. Ever since I read her note, I keep thinking about how I felt at her age. The things that didn't matter, but I thought they did. The things that *did* matter that I ignored. Like my dad."

Ty watched her, listening in that way he had. Making her feel heard when she wasn't even sure she was making *sense.*

"I was always ashamed of him. Of my mom, too, for that matter. Because she *enabled* his crazy. At least that's how it seemed to me. I thought his ideas were stupid. Who in the hell needed or wanted a damn feet dryer? Or an automated hairbrush cleaner? Or any of the ideas he had for kitchens. You don't even want to know what some of them were."

"Great minds are hard to understand."

"I know. Even then, I knew that."

"So are you beating yourself up because you didn't appreciate his genius? Or is something else going on?"

"He never even came close to seeing one of his ideas become more. Not once. I guess, standing where I am . . . knowing that I'm on the brink of a breakthrough . . . it makes me wonder how he survived all that disappointment. All the naysayers. Me."

"Dreams come in different shapes and sizes, Kari. Maybe you're looking through the wrong lens."

Her head came up. "What do you mean?"

"For you, it's the golden ring. Grabbing it. Keeping it. That's what you want, right?"

She nodded, but she knew a bigger message was coming. She wasn't sure that she wanted to hear it, though.

"For your dad, maybe it was the vision that fulfilled him. Knowing he'd thought of something no one else had."

Kari paused, staring at him while his words sunk in. She'd never considered it that way before, never looked at it through that particular lens. And something inside gave, like a tight band that suddenly snapped, letting her take a deep breath for the first time in a long time.

"Maybe to your dad, it didn't matter if anyone else valued what he'd made," Ty finished softly.

"Even when it mattered to the people who loved him?"

"Love shouldn't have contingencies," he said, brows pulled together, as if he questioned himself even as he spoke.

She took a deep breath, knowing that his own father had entered the conversation. It pained her to see the hurt their estrangement caused. Not just because it was pointless, but because she'd give anything to be able to see her parents again, to tell her father she was sorry she hadn't understood his genius. To tell her mother thank you for caring so much for them both. Ty's dad lived less than a handful of miles away and yet it might as well have been light years.

"Have you told your dad that, Ty?" she asked

softly.

He leveled a steady gaze at her, but his eyes were shuttered and she had no idea what he was thinking.

"I know you want to help, Kari. But this thing between me and my dad? It's been years in the making. You're not going to solve it in the next—what do you have? Twenty days?"

He never raised his voice or edged it with anger, but his words hit her like a slap, and she had to look away. She didn't want him to see how badly he'd hurt her.

Their food arrived, saving her from a response while the waiter served them. But a pot had been stirred and neither of them knew what to do with the thickening broth.

CHAPTER SIXTEEN

TY COULDN'T PINPOINT exactly when he'd fallen in love with her. Maybe it was that first moment when she'd walked through the door like a spring breeze, confident, vibrant, and so very beautiful. Whenever it happened, he was in deep. Now, the calendar has become his enemy. He'd known from the start that it would come down to this—this gut wrenching feeling of the inevitable. And he had no one to blame but himself. She'd tried to make a clean break. But even in the beginning, he couldn't let her go.

Now that he knew her . . . The complexities of her thoughts, her desires . . . he only loved her more.

They hardly spoke after they left the restaurant. And their lovemaking had a desperate edge to it that lacerated his already overworked thoughts. She lay curled against him, her head on his chest, hand low on his belly, stroking the skin there, lost in thought.

"Why do you think the card you chose from the Wish Tree was meant for you?" he asked softly.

He'd been thinking of it ever since she brought it up, knowing that a deeper meaning had been rooted in her concerns. Grasping at it like a ledge over a bottomless pit.

"Because she doesn't know what she really wants," Kari said without hesitation.

As soon as the words were out, he felt her stiffen, as if saying it out loud had finally exposed the secret meaning. Did she understand the parallel? Or would she remain stubbornly blind to it?

"What do you think she really wants?" he asked.

"I'm not sure," she answered, wariness in her tone. "She didn't *ask* for anything for herself. Not outright. But she longs to fit in so much . . . . I bought her this outfit that I know she'll love. It's trendy—what every other teenaged girl will be wearing. But giving it to her feels like . . . I don't know. A sign that she's *supposed* to change, make herself fit in."

He waited, silently urging her to keep talking. Whatever point she was headed for, he knew it would expose something he needed to know.

"But she doesn't. And she won't, just because she's wearing the right clothes, or saying the right thing. All she'll be doing is pretending. And if I give her this *gift*, I feel like I'll be guiding her down that path." She laughed softly, sadly. "I guess I have illusions of grandeur. It's just a Christmas present, after all."

"From a tree that's meant to make wishes come true," he said. "That's a powerful thing."

She was still a moment, then she tipped her face up and looked at him. "So what do I do?"

"Let her know she has a choice. She thinks she wants to be normal. You think the things that make her different are what makes her special."

Kari sat up and stared at him with wide eyes. "Yes."

"So send her the message that she gets to choose. That all of us, get to choose. Whatever path you're on, you can get off."

He wasn't talking about Sara anymore and Kari knew it.

"But that's a lie. Just like you said with your dad. Your choice is to let the past go and reconnect. His choice is to hold onto it and stay apart."

He came up on his elbow and locked eyes with her. "What about your choices, Kari?"

"I don't have choices. I have a plan."

"Plans can change."

Her eyes glistened and her bottom lip looked shaky. She bit it and shook her head. "I'm two feet from gold, Ty. Close enough to touch everything I've dreamed of, worked for. Want."

"But where does that leave us?"

Her lashes came down, but not before he saw the panic in her eyes. "I thought . . . I know it's crazy, but I thought we could try the long distance thing. Wherever my next step takes me, we could find a way—"

"No," he said, touching her face with his fingertips, aching inside. He cupped her jaw and closed his eyes. "You know that won't work. Not for us."

"Why?" she asked in a broken voice.

"We're all or nothing, sweetheart. Have been since the start."

"I don't want to say goodbye to you, Ty," she whispered.

"Then don't."

"But, you said it yourself. The reason you came home, your dad, it isn't working out. Pack your bags. You and I could make—"

"No," he said again, though it felt like cutting out his own heart. "This is my home. It's a part of me. What I do here, teaching. That's part of me, too."

"You wouldn't have to stop teaching."

"It's not just that, sweetheart. I don't want to be baggage, and eventually, I would be. You'd call me your anchor, but I'd feel like a ball and chain. I can't live on the kind of plan you have in your head. I can't sit by and watch you work yourself to death for something I know you don't really want."

She pulled back. That had stung. He'd meant it to. "What's that supposed to mean?"

"This dream of yours. It's not about proving yourself. Landing the big deal. Money. You're trying to compensate for something you think is missing in you. Something I know you already have."

"What's that?"

He stood up, though getting out of her bed was one of the hardest things he'd ever done. "You're like Sara, sweetheart. How can you not see that? You want this thing—this intangible, unattainable *thing*. Success, to compensate for your dad's failures. Documented plans that can prove you're worth what you've achieved. Numbers, lining up the way they should. But that's not what you really want. You want something that will free you. That will blast away the power your fear has over you. You want to risk it all and be happy with whatever happens."

She stared at him, her mouth open, her brows pulled tight. She didn't like what he'd said, but she'd needed to hear it. Really, *hear it*.

"I'm not afraid," she said in a wooden tone.

He let out a deep breath, and shook his head. She was, and they both knew it.

"You need to make up your mind, Kari. Do you want the cool kid's clothes? Or do you want to stand out and be yourself, warts and all?"

Her eyes were filled with anger, confusion, hurt. All the things he was feeling himself.

"I want to be with you, Kari. I'm in *love* with you. I don't care if you're Entrepreneur of the Year or you decide to sell hot dogs on the corner. And I don't think you care either. Not really. Not deep down."

Her lips moved silently over the word love. He couldn't tell if she was giving it back or simply trying it out.

He fished his clothes out of the tangle on the floor and pulled on his briefs, then his jeans. Kari watched with widening eyes.

"You know where to find me when you make up your mind."

"Wait. You're leaving?"

"I'm going home. I didn't choose to come back just for my dad. I came back for me. I love being a part of community. *This* community. I want to live here, in a place where people know me. Where the work I do matters to the people I do it for. I want to settle down. Maybe raise a family here. And no, I'm not walking away from my father just because he's a pain in the ass. I'm not walking away from you, either. I want to be with you, Kari. But not if it means I've got to hold on so tight you can't get loose."

"You want . . . ."

"You. I want you, Kari Dale. I'm willing to fight for you, too. But I meant what I said. I won't be the consolation prize. The thing you got because you didn't make it up, up and away."

He shut his mouth before the pain of leaving her made him say more. Made him abandon his resolve, ignore what he knew was right, and climb right back in bed with her. While she watched with a stunned expression, he finished dressing, pulled on his boots, and grabbed his coat.

Before he walked out the door, he took her face between his hands and kissed her, pouring everything he felt into it.

"Choose me," he said.

She blinked her tearful eyes at him, but she didn't say the words he wanted to hear. She didn't say anything, which was answer enough. He'd put it all out there, but Kari had plans. He couldn't even feel cheated as he left her house for the lonely drive home. She'd told him from the start that she'd be long gone come the New Year.

He just hadn't realized she'd be taking such a big part of him with her.

CHAPTER SEVENTEEN

THE CALL FROM Leimann's came the week before Christmas. Eight days after Ty had walked out on her. Everything that had happened since had been marked by that point of no return.

Simone answered the phone at seven thirty in the morning. Both women had arrived early to work on the books and prepare their deposits. Their desks faced one another—it was the only configuration the small office would allow—so Kari heard both sides of the conversation. She could have scripted the first part from her daydreams of how this call would go.

Them: We've been watching the success of your stores. We think you have your finger on the pulse of the young male buyer.

Us: We've worked very hard to see our vision become reality.

Them: We'd like to take your brand to the next level. We've put together an offer we think you'll want to entertain.

Us: We're listening.

After Simone hung up, the two women stared at one another in shock.

"Did that just happen?" Simone asked.

Just like in the movies. Everything they'd wished for was about to come true.

A representative from their corporate office showed up to negotiate terms the next day. Forty-eight hours later, the written offer arrived via a FedEx driver. Henry Timberlake was in the store at the time, flirting with Simone as she helped him pick out "new duds" for his date with Becky Smith.

"She makes me feel like a young man again," he said.

"You look like a young man," Simone teased. "I wouldn't put you a day over forty."

Henry laughed at that, but when the delivery man walked through the door as Simone rung up his purchases, Henry grew quiet and watchful. He couldn't miss the look of excitement that passed between the two women.

"Good news?" he said.

"Leimann's Department Stores wants to buy us out," Simone blurted.

"The bastards," Henry said, mistaking the intent for a hostile takeover.

"No—it's good. They want all five stores—well the stock anyway. They don't plan to keep the bricks and mortar."

Henry frowned, still not following. Kari said nothing. The churning emotions inside her were too sharp, too confusing.

"They'll shut you down?" Henry asked.

"No. They'll take our brand and make it theirs. Make it big. And they're going to pay us a whole lot of money to do it."

"You're selling out? You're selling your store?"

"That was always the plan," Simone said.

Henry shut his mouth with a snap and turned shocked eyes to Kari. "You knew about this?" he demanded.

Simone, so caught up in her excitement that she missed the tension, answered for her. "It was Kari's plan. Her *brilliant* plan. Make the brand, sell it for big bucks, move on."

Henry was still staring at her. "Move on?" he repeated. "What about my son? Does he know about this?"

Kari felt like her heart was lodged somewhere in her throat. She couldn't speak. Not when it hurt so much. Why hadn't she seen this coming, this plunging, *too late to turn back now*, feeling?

"Does he?" Henry demanded.

Kari nodded.

"Son of a bitch," Henry muttered. He swiped his bag off the counter, gave them both a tip of his hat and stomped out the door.

Simone watched him go with a stunned expression. "Why is he so pissed?"

It could be any number of reasons. He'd finally sold his family legacy, only to have it shut down with no prospect of anything replacing it. But that hadn't been his first concern. No, it had been Ty. His son—the one he wouldn't even speak to.

Simone looked perplexed as she studied Kari's face. "What's going on here, Kari? Aren't you happy about this offer? Isn't this what you wanted?"

Numb, Kari nodded. "Yes. It's what I wanted."

Except now . . . now . . . .

"Okay," Simone said, not really convinced. "I'll send their contract over to Jake to review." Jake was her brother and their lawyer. "I'm sure he'll want some changes. But I feel like celebrating! How about you?"

"I do, Simone. I promise. But there are a couple of things I need to take care of today. Can I have a raincheck?"

"Kari, what is going *on?* Why aren't you as happy as I am? Is it Ty? I thought you two split up?"

"We did. But . . . I just need some time to process. Okay? Please? I'll get there. I promise."

"Tell me you're not thinking of walking away from this deal."

"I'm not. I swear. I wouldn't do that to you, Simone."

And she wouldn't. But now that the time had come to claim the success she'd worked so hard for, all Kari wanted to do was cry.

She didn't though. If she let even one tear fall, she feared she'd never stop.

Stoic and dry eyed, she dug out her to-do list. Today was the last day to deliver her gifts to the Wish Tree before they were picked up for disbursement to the many children. And having a purpose gave her the strength to ignore the chaos of her emotions. It wouldn't last though. Like an avalanche rumbling in the distance, the landslide of feelings was just waiting to come down on her.

She drove to Big Sky Living and the Wish Tree, braving the storm that had swept down from the mountains. It powdered the streets and buffered all sound. It echoed the numbness she felt inside.

With the free time that Ty's absence had left her, she'd thought about what he said. About Sara. About choices. And finally she'd figured out what to get the young woman. She'd wrapped all four boxes—one each for the younger kids, stuffed with the items they'd requested, plus some extras she thought they might enjoy. Sara had two boxes wrapped together and a card, from Kari to Sara. Kari had cried when she'd written it. She hoped it would speak to Sara's heart.

She left the boxes with the efficient elf who checked off the children's names in her book. "Thank you for sharing the spirit of Christmas," the elf told her.

Kari had tears in her eyes as she murmured, "Merry Christmas."

As she turned, she found Santa standing right behind her. He smiled his jolly smile at her. "Merry Christmas."

"Merry Christmas to you, too," she said, less enthusiastically. And then, because she had to know, "I was here a few weeks ago . . . ."

"I remember you, Kari Dale."

His use of her name cut off her words. "How do

you know who I am?"

He winked. "Santa Claus."

"Oh. Right. That makes sense."

On Mars, maybe.

"I just wondered about the cards you had in your bag . . . They all say *your wish is granted*, right?"

He smiled again. "Is that what you're hoping for?"

Vexed, she shook her head. "I just want to know."

"Why? Will it make your wish coming true any less important?"

"No. I mean, you don't even know what I want."

He laughed again, a jolly chuckle that crinkled his eyes and jiggled his belly. "Ah, Kari. It's you who doesn't know. You haven't figured that out, yet?"

She opened her mouth, but didn't answer. Because no, dammit, evidently she hadn't.

"Go see your teacher, Kari. He knows what he wants, but without you he can't have it."

Stunned didn't describe how she felt. Hit by a truck came closer.

She made it to her car without breaking down, but as soon as the door closed, she couldn't hold it any longer. Great, heaving sobs rose up from deep within her as she let everything she'd managed to suppress since he walked out the door rise to the surface.

She missed Ty so much that each day without him seemed bleak and endless. And the thought of a future that didn't include him? She couldn't bear it.

The cheerful Christmas music playing in the parking lot jarred her already aching heart. The goodwill of the people bustling around her—some of them people she'd come to know—it all felt like salt in an open wound.

Her emotions had been twisted up since she'd met Ty. They'd been in shreds since he told her that he loved her.

And then walked out the door. Out of her life.

Choose me, he'd said.

At first, she'd been angry. How dare he deliver such an ultimatum? But it hadn't taken long for that to burn off and reality to step in. He'd said, *choose me.* Not, *quit you job or give up your dreams.* He'd simply asked her to add him to those dreams.

There was no real reason why she had to leave. The offer on the table wasn't contingent on her packing her bags and moving on. She didn't have to keep living a nomad's life. She could end this self-inflicted isolation with just a word to the right man.

And he was the right man. In her heart, she knew that. He was the only man as far as she was concerned. It had just taken this painful moment to understand.

She wiped her tears and started the car. She would go to him, beg him to take her back if that's what it took. And she would do it now.

CHAPTER EIGHTEEN

TY WAS HAVING a hell of a time focusing on his class, and they knew it. And, like the pack animals they were, the room full of teenagers had immediately spotted the weakness and began to work it. Josh had asked for the bathroom pass four times. Daniel couldn't keep his trap shut and Miley, Suzie and Coralynn Whitney—cousins, not triplets, thank God—giggled at every smartass comment he made. Normally, Ty could appreciate his wit. The kid was funny. Today, not so much.

"All right," Ty said, rapping a book on his desk to get their attention. "I know it's the last day before Winter Break. I know you're all excited Santa Claus is coming, and you're ready to blow out those doors, right now. But I can't let you out for another forty-two minutes and I don't have the patience for your shenanigans."

Wrong word to use. He knew it as soon as he uttered the first syllable.

"Shenanigans," Josh repeated derisively.

"You sure you want to use that tone with me?" Ty said.

Josh shut his mouth.

"Okay," he said with a deep breath. "Let's make these last interminable minutes of school as painless as possible. I have potentially valuable prizes for right answers. Who is—"

His classroom door burst open and Ty's dad stomped inside. Ty gaped at him for a full count, before he managed to sputter, "Dad? What are you doin—"

"Did you know?" Henry Timberlake interrupted. "Did you know she was just going to use the store and then *sell* it?"

He could only be talking about Kari. In truth, Ty had been waiting for someone to spring the news on him. He just hadn't expected it to come from his dad. Yet with the snow and the good cheer and that little white card he'd been carrying around like a love sick boy—*your wish has been granted*—he'd hoped.

He'd hoped she'd choose him.

"She's really leaving?" he said numbly.

"Leimann's Department Stores bought her out," Henry spat. "Now she's moving on. Who cares about Timberlake's? Certainly, not you."

"When?" Ty asked.

"Sounded like it just happened. I can't believe you didn't say something, if you knew."

Ty gave a bitter laugh. "To you? You didn't even tell me you'd sold the place. You haven't had a nice word for me in years. Why in the hell would I come to you with anything?"

A collective gasp whispered through the classroom. Profanity—loved by all teens—was against SBHS's zero tolerance rules.

"Sorry," he said.

"We got your back, Mr. T," Josh assured him.

Henry looked at Josh and the rest of the class with surprise. Had he taken the roomful of students for cardboard cutouts? Of course, they were listening.

"You're Johnson Riley's oldest, aren't you?" Henry said, eyeing Josh suspiciously.

Josh nodded.

"He can't keep his nose out of other people's business either. You can tell him I said so, too."

"Dad," Ty said. "Dial it down."

Henry scowled. "Are you just going to let her pack her bags and go away?"

Again, no doubts who he meant.

"It was her choice."

And she'd chosen her dreams. He got that.

Didn't stop it from hurting like hell, though.

"I thought I raised you better than that," Henry said.

"Better than to respect a woman's choices?"

"Better than to stand there with your head up your—" He paused, looked at the avid audience and scowled some more. "Don't you all have better things to do? Get out your homework or something."

"There's no homework," Josh said. "It's the day before Winter Break, man."

And there were still thirty-two minutes of class to go. They were going to be long ones, too.

"Dad," Ty said, interrupting before this got completely out of hand. "I have class and, as you can see, they're eager to listen up and learn something. If you want to talk, let's have dinner. Now, is not the time or place."

And that's when the door flew open again and yet another unexpected visitor burst into the room.

CHAPTER NINETEEN

THE DRIVE FROM the Wish Tree to the high school wasn't far, but the snow, made the freshly plowed streets slushy and slick. Fat, bedazzled flakes flurried from a sky so low, it seemed mystical. Kari's wipers worked overtime, but couldn't begin to combat the silent attack. She was white-knuckled by the time she pulled into visitor parking. Filled with the overwhelming fear that she'd waited too long to figure things out, that she'd better hurry or she'd be too late, Kari jumped out of the car and sprinted across the lot until she hit an icy patch and almost ended up on her ass.

She took a moment, a breath, and then calmly—carefully—made her way to the door. The holiday decorations looked a little worse for the wear, but the counter just inside the office had three plates of cookies next to a boom-box merrily playing *Cossack Dance* from the *Nutcracker*. The music had an urgent beat Kari felt deep inside her

Marianne looked up when Kari walked in. Kari remembered the first time she'd been to the school, the wild butterflies whirling in her stomach, and how warm and friendly Marianne's smile had been when she'd greeted her.

Marianne eyed her now, and Kari knew things were going to go a bit differently today. In her head, she heard Ty say, *Small town, sweetheart. Nothing happens here that someone doesn't know about.*

"Merry Christmas," Marianne said with all the warmth of a snowball in the face.

Because Kari was the out-of-town wench who'd seduced the hometown hero then cast him aside.

"Merry Christmas," Kari answered, irrationally struck with an ache in her chest. She didn't know Marianne well enough to miss her smile. "I'm here to see Ty."

Nonplussed, Marianne said, "I guessed."

Right. Why else?

"He's teaching right now. You can wait if you want."

And her expression said, *Until hell freezes over and starts handing out donuts. What kind of idiot breaks up with Ty Timberlake?*

"You're right," Kari said, horrified when she realized she'd said it out loud. "I mean, why did I think staying with Ty was the wrong decision?"

Good grief. She had tears in her voice. Tears in her eyes. She probably sounded like a crazy person, too. Marianne's brows came down suspiciously.

The sound of a deep voice raised in anger rumbled from the down the hall. It came from the direction of Ty's classroom, but it wasn't Ty's voice.

"Mr. T's dad is here, too," Marianne said

grudgingly.

"His dad?" Kari repeated. "Here? You said Ty was teaching."

Kari didn't wait for a response. She started down the hall. If Henry was here, fighting with Ty in the middle of class, she'd be damned if she'd wait for permission to go in, too.

"Hey! You can't go back there," Marianne said, scrambling from behind her desk to follow.

While the *Nutcracker* music rose to a crescendo, Kari took off in a sprint.

"Stop," Marianne hollered, trying to catch up. "I said you—Wait just a minute! If you don't stop, I'll call Security."

The school security guard was outside, walking the perimeter. He'd waved to Kari when she'd pulled in. No way he'd be back in time to stop her.

With Marianne charging behind her, Kari raced down the hall. She could hear Henry's voice, muffled but booming as she neared Ty's door.

"Are you just going to let her pack her bags and go away?"

Marianne had gained on her. The sound of their running feet drowned out Ty's response, while in her head, the Nutcracker's relentless *bum da-da-da-da bum-dum-dum, bum da-da-da-da bum-dum-dum* played on.

Just before Marianne's reaching fingers found Kari's arm, Kari burst into Ty's room, panting, sweaty, tear stained and without a clue about what she planned to say. Marianne stumbled in a second latter, red-faced and out of breath.

A classroom full of teenagers gawked at them. They weren't alone. Ty stared at her like she'd just beamed in from another planet, and beside him, Henry wore an identical expression. Both of their mouths were open, but neither one of them had figured out what they wanted to say yet. If not for Marianne's labored breathing, the silence would have been complete.

"I tried to stop her," Marianne managed, sucking wind like they'd run a five-mile race instead of a fifty-yard dash.

"It's fine," Ty said, regaining his composure before the rest of them. "I'll escort her back out in a minute. Thank you, Marianne. I've got it from here."

At Ty's smooth dismissal, Marianne shot Kari a poisonous look and about-faced. She didn't close the door behind her and her footsteps echoed back reproachfully. Henry stayed where he was. So did Kari. Ty's students watched with undivided attention.

Way to go, Kari.

A hasty exit would be the smart course of action, but Kari's brain had taken a back seat to the rising lump of emotion caught somewhere between heart and throat. She had things to say and they needed to be said now, like *right now*. If that meant she'd be spilling her guts in front of Ty, a room full of hormonal teenagers, and one crusty old man, so be it.

She took a deep breath, squared her shoulders and opened mouth.

"Wait," Ty said.

CHAPTER TWENTY

THE SIGHT OF Kari standing in his room, disheveled, face streaked from tears, and eyes glittering with emotions he wasn't sure he believed, had completely caught him off guard. First his dad, busting in like he had every right. Now, the woman he couldn't stop thinking of. Whatever came down next, he didn't need the audience.

He faced the class. "You all go home," he said to them.

No one moved. Nineteen minutes of class remained and, technically, Ty wasn't allowed to dismiss them early. It was a hard, fast rule that had been implemented twelve years ago when an early release had resulted in the vandalism of the library and one broken nose. Letting class out early could be counted as grounds for termination. Ty didn't even care.

"I said, go home," he said in his *don't question my authority* voice.

Still, no one was willing to give up their front row seats to what promised to be the most exciting thing to ever happen at Starlight Bend High.

Josh—who else?—interrupted the silence and

blurted, "You've been getting with *her*? *Damn*, Mr. T."

The tone held such respect that Ty nearly smiled. The kid didn't know the half of it. Kari was everything he didn't know he wanted. Needed. Craved like air. But if his dad was right, Kari already had her ticket out of town. She was either here to say goodbye or try one last time to convince him to go with her.

Either way, he refused to have the conversation in front of his students.

If he couldn't get rid of them, though, maybe he could count on his dad, for once in his life.

"Dad. Would you mind babysitting my class for a few minutes while I have a word with Kari?"

Henry looked at him like he'd sprouted fangs and meant to use them. "Me? Hell, no. I'm not watching these monsters."

A collective gasp came from the students. Whether it was the profanity or the slur, Ty wasn't sure.

"Students, Dad," Ty corrected angrily.

"I don't care what you call them. I came here for a reason and it's got nothing to do with watching your . . . class."

"What are you so damn mad about, old man?" Josh demanded.

Another gasp. Ty looked heavenward, praying for strength.

"Language and respect, Josh. That's your only warning."

But the kid had asked a good question. One Ty had asked many times before. But for some reason, this time, in this place, Henry decided to answer.

"What am I mad about?" Henry repeated, red-faced, eyes blazing. "You want to know what I'm *mad* about? What really gets under my bonnet?"

Josh snickered at that, but Kari leaned forward. "Yes," she said. "I, for one, would really like to know. What grudge have you been nurturing all these years, Henry? Why can't you just accept Ty for the great man he is?"

God, she was sweet and loyal to a fault. But she had no idea what she'd stumbled into here, what decrepit reasoning Henry was about to toss out to the crowd. Ty needed to do some damage control before this bad situation became mayhem.

"Get out your books," he said to the class. "Chapter Eleven. No one leaves this room until I have five hundred words about how Montana achieved statehood."

"Your lack of responsibility," Henry said, before anyone had a chance to obey. Not that Ty was fooling himself that they would.

"You just quit this family," Henry spat.

"I didn't quit the damn family, dad."

On cue, the students gasped again. Three—no four—swear words in one class. A few of the kids looked worried for him.

"You took off when you wanted," Henry went on, too wound up to care about anything but speaking his mind. "You came back when you wanted. I'd be a fool to think you won't take off again the next time *you* feel like it. *You.* Doesn't matter to *you* what anyone else wants."

The unfairness of it rolled over Ty like snowplow. "Come on, Dad," he said, no longer caring who heard. "How long are you going to blame me for growing up?"

"Plenty of boys have grown into men right here in this town," Henry shouted.

"Maybe they have," Ty shouted back. "But I needed to get away from the crazy, Dad. You and grandpa and mom. Jesus, it was like living in a war zone."

"Your grandad was a good man."

"He was a mean, angry bastard," Ty corrected. That one didn't even get a gasp from the students. "He taught you how to be hard. He taught you that forgiveness is fake and you can't trust the people you love. He drove a wedge between you and mom and between you and me."

"I make no apology for who I am," Henry said proudly, hearing only what he chose to hear. As usual. "And you won't catch me blaming my parents for all of my problems. That's what your generation does. Not mine. Millennials," he said with disgust.

"He's no millennial," Josh interjected. *"We're* millennials."

Ty glanced at Josh, stunned that he even knew the word, let alone how to apply it. "You're Gen Z," Ty corrected. "But nice use of vocabulary."

Henry opened his mouth again, but Kari cut him off.

"Stop it," she said softly. "Do you even hear

yourselves? You're fighting over something that happened years ago. What's it matter now? You're the only family you have left. Why do you make the past more important than the future?"

"Family sticks together," Henry said stubbornly. "Stays together."

"But you're the one who's keeping your family apart," Kari insisted. "Ty came back to connect with you, and all of you've done is push him away even more."

"Well, coming from someone like you," Henry muttered.

"Meaning what?" Ty demanded.

"She sold us out," Henry said mulishly.

"She has the right to do what she wants. The world doesn't revolve around you, believe it or not."

"Doesn't revolve around you, either, Tyler."

"Come on, Dad," Ty said. "What do you want? You want me to pretend that leaving wasn't the right thing for me? Did you really want me to spend my life never knowing what else there is? Running a hardware store that I don't care about? Was that the future you saw for me?"

"Don't you mock my life's work," Henry said. "And I'd appreciate you not airing our woes in front of her." Henry jabbed a finger in Kari's direction. "And them," he tacked on.

"*Her*?" Ty exclaimed. "Trust me. She knows more about all this than either one of us ever could."

"You talk about our business to a stranger?"

Ty laughed. "Number one, you knocked down my door to air *our business* in front of a classroom full of teenagers. Marianne is probably out there tweeting about every damn thing we say. Number two, I don't have to share what I'm thinking with Kari. She's had me figured out since the moment she laid eyes on me."

"I wish," Kari muttered.

"She's female, Dad," Ty went on when Henry didn't seem to get the point. "She smarter than us both."

The girls in the class high-fived. The boys looked bewildered. Definite skepticism lowered Henry's brows and he seemed completely disinclined to back down. If anything, his eyes looked a little wild, now.

"You know," Kari said, speaking softly, making everyone quiet down to hear. "I can't even remember my dad's face. When I close my eyes and try to call the memory? I can't see him at all. I can hear his laugh, though. He had a big one. Loud as all get-out. A little phlegmy—the smoking—but like a summer storm. You could hear it coming in the distance. It never failed to make others smile along."

Everyone was watching her, even the two students in the back who'd been asleep earlier. Ty saw her note their avid attention, but she didn't back off. That mutinous chin of hers went up, and she stared Henry, right in the eye.

"When was the last time you made your son laugh, Henry? Or even smile? When was the last time you told him you loved him, or that you were proud of him? What do you think he's going to remember when you're gone?"

She turned to Ty. "And you? You came all the way out here to be closer to him, but you never took that last step. You never got closer. He pushed you away, and you just let him. I've only known you a couple of months, but you're a man who gets what he wants. I know that much. So what's your excuse?"

She hadn't come here to talk about his relationship with his dad. He knew that in his gut. But the passion in her voice, the hurt in her eyes . . . it moved him. Shamed him, because she was right. He'd come back and called it good enough. Made overtures, sure. But he figured if his dad wanted anything more, he'd have to meet Ty halfway. Deep down, though, he'd known Henry wouldn't. He'd told himself that he'd done his part by coming home. Why had it taken Kari to make him see his own failure?

"I would give anything to hear my dad laugh again," she said. "Anything."

In the silence that cloaked the room, strains of *I'll Be Home for Christmas* drifted down from the office. Marianne and Principal Baker had probably broken out the eggnog and cookies as they listened to the true confessions coming out of Ty's classroom.

"I'll never have that chance," Kari went on. "But you two are right here, in the same town. And it's *Christmas*, for God's sake. Whatever is keeping you apart, you need to fix it. Fix it now."

Her words resonated deep within him. He met his father's eyes and saw that she'd managed to penetrate

Henry's thick crust as well.

"Dad," he began, when a piercing, electronic shriek cut through the silence. The sound was loud, obviously unexpected, and coming from Kari's purse.

Kari froze, a stricken expression on her face. For a moment, it seemed she didn't understand what the sound meant any more than Ty did. The shriek came again, twice this time, and Kari jumped.

"Oh my God," she breathed, opening the big purse she carried as it went off again—three screeches this time.

"Is that your phone?" Lora, a student who had to be told repeatedly to put her phone away, asked in a condescending tone.

"No, no, no" Kari said, rummaging through God knew what that she carried in that bag. As it sounded off a fourth time, she grasped something and yanked it out.

The thing in her hand was about a half inch thick and three in circumference—roughly the size of a hockey puck, but bright red and glowing. A light flashed frantically at the top.

"What in the devil is that?" Henry asked.

"A fire alarm," she said, eyes wide. "It's one of my dad's inventions. It's hooked up to the phone and the smoke detectors in the store."

Ty caught on quicker than his father. "The hardware store's on fire? You sure? Is anyone there?"

"Yes. No. I mean, we closed early on account of the offer. That's why I'm here." She still held the alarm in her hand, shaking her head. "I wasn't even sure it worked," she said. "But with my history, I hooked it up anyway . . . ."

"What history?" Henry demanded.

"Never mind," Ty said, taking Kari's arm as he pulled out his phone. Now all the students took action, jumping from their seats as if to follow.

"Absolutely not," Ty shouted. "Sit down."

At that moment, Principal Baker rounded the corner. "Marianne said an alarm was going off."

"Fire at the hardware store," Ty said. "Can you watch my class?"

"Was just about to announce early dismissal. This storm isn't letting up. You'll have a time getting anywhere in it. Be careful."

CHAPTER TWENTY-ONE

PRINCIPAL BAKER'S PREDICTION turned out to be accurate.

Kari sat in the front on the bench seat, sandwiched in between father and son as Ty navigated the treacherous roads with both hands on the wheel. While she'd been at the school, the skies had simply opened up and dropped several feet of snow—all at once; everywhere. It came down so fast and furious that Kari couldn't see two feet in front of her. She didn't know if Ty kept the truck on the road or not, because she couldn't even see the road. She'd stuffed the screeching, flashing PA—Pocket Alarm, though it was too big for a pocket—back into her purse and put it under the seat, but every thirty seconds it shrieked, keeping them all on edge.

She'd called Simone as soon as they'd left the school and broken the news.

"Don't worry," Simone said. "Even if the whole place burns down, it won't impact our deal. We hardly have any merchandise left anyway. The damage will be minimal."

Kari knew it was true. And the deal Leimann's

offered was for the brand they'd built and the designer contacts they'd made—even if they lost everything on the shelves, it would only be a blip. But her worries were for the businesses on either side of the store. What if they caught fire, too?

Starlight Bend's fire department was a volunteer organization, but they'd assembled like pros and were already there by the time Ty pulled up to the store.

"The fire's out," the Chief—who also happened to be Stan, the cantankerous bartender—told them. "Looks like the old Timberlake sign shorted out, started an electrical burn. Most of the damage is in the ceiling and the kitchen. How'd you even know it was burning? No one's here and Ed's place next door closed down yesterday so he could go see his daughter in Pittsburg, Elaina on the other side left town last week."

Numb, relieved, and feeling that somewhere in this snowy, freezing storm there was another sign that she'd somehow missed, Kari pulled out the flashing PA. She'd finally managed to quiet the screeching, but not shut off the lights.

"My dad invented it. It's like a pager. It goes off when the smoke detectors do."

And not only had it *worked,* it was one of the few things her father had actually patented. She hadn't been the only one in the family who'd had troubles with things bursting into flames.

Stan asked if he could see it and was soon surrounded by other firefighters, discussing the contraption. After a moment, one of them tromped inside, and the bleeping smoke detector shut off. A few seconds later, the PA quit flashing.

"Thank God," Kari muttered.

"That little thing there, it might have saved this whole street," Stan said. "You should sell them."

With a brisk nod, he joined his comrades in packing up the fire truck. Henry had gone inside to inspect the damage. Now, he came back out. "Couldn't even tell there was a fire if you didn't know what to look for. Except in the kitchen, and it was worse for the wear anyway. Smells smoky back there, too, but I don't think any of your fancy jeans are ruined. A little airing out is all that's needed."

The three of them stood in the shelter of the entryway, shivering and uncertain about what to do next.

Finally, Henry said, "You used some pretty strong words earlier, missy. I guess you have to when you're talking to someone who's got a hard head. I want you to know I heard you."

He cleared his throat and faced his son. "This here isn't the place. The way I see it, you need to settle other business first anyway." His pointed glance at Kari left her in no doubt what that other business was. "But after you get that squared away, maybe we could have a drink. Cup of coffee. Whatever."

"I'd like that, Dad."

Henry nodded, his eyes over-bright. "Fight the good fight, son," he said with another glance at Kari. Then he joined the fireman as they climbed aboard the truck. "Think I could hitch a ride home?"

CHAPTER TWENTY-TWO

THEY WERE BOTH quiet when they entered Ty's house. There'd been no question about where they would go. Kari's rental was too far away and the storm too fierce to make the journey. Every business in town had closed down. The wind and snow owned the world now.

Ty's house was warm. When he turned on the light to combat the murky shadows, the Christmas tree came on too, sparkling happily in the corner. Buttercup dashed out to say hello, her floppy ears and wagging tail a welcome sight. Kari knelt down to show her some love while Ty shed his coat, turned on the coffee maker, and immediately started a fire in the hearth.

When she looked up, Ty was watching her.

"I know what you came to the school to tell me," he said, surprising her. "And it wasn't anything about my dad. You're leaving. You made your choice."

Still on her knees with Buttercup in her arms, she nodded, stopped. Shook her head. "I don't want to leave."

Her voice wavered over the words, betraying her feelings. She felt naked, exposed, and so very afraid of what he'd say next.

"What?"

"You were right about me. I came here—to Starlight Bend—with one goal, Ty. Launch. That's it. Launch the business. Launch myself to the next stage, whatever it might be. But that day we met, I think I started to change right then. And I don't think our meeting was an accident or just a fluke. It was fate. I *needed* to meet you. I needed an anchor, if only for a minute. I've been riding the waves from one point to another, thinking I was getting what I wanted. Working to reach something I thought would be meaningful. But when the call came in and we got the buyout offer—I wasn't even happy. And it made me realize that I haven't been happy in a very long time. Except when I'm with you. You make me happy."

He stared at her, his expression closed, his eyes alert, but shuttered.

"Yes, you ground me," she rushed on. "But you also help me see everything that I've missed because I've been moving too fast. You make me enjoy living. You've made me see that I took . . . I took my memory of my parents and somehow twisted it all up into this . . . *plan* of mine. This *Rule the World* strategy that I thought would set me apart—make me different, *better* than they were. But that's not what I want, deep down." She placed her hands over her heart. "Here."

"What do you want, Kari?"

"You. All of you. I'm in love with you Ty. Can't you see that?"

He narrowed his eyes, shook his head.

"I'm sorry it took so long for me to figure it out. I just thought I had to choose. You or me." She sniffed, smiling through her tears. "I know how stupid that sounds. I just couldn't see how to make it work, though."

"And now?"

"Now, I can. Loving you doesn't mean I can't still be me. Yes, I want to create something. Something sustainable. Something *real*. I still want to succeed. I still want to be the best. But I want a life, too." Her voice cracked again. "I want a life with *you*, Ty. Here, in this little town that has magic on every corner. I want to contribute and be *known*. I want to be known as the woman who belongs with you."

"Why?" he asked simply.

"Because I love you. Because you already know more about me than I do about myself. These past few days without you? I've never been so miserable in my life."

Ty let out a sigh and looked away. Kari felt as if her world had just opened up beneath her feet and she was sliding down, sliding into the swirling miasma of a life that couldn't be complete. Not without Ty.

"I'm too late, aren't I?" she said.

Ty shook his head and gave a soft laugh. "I fell in love with you in about ten minutes, Kari. But I don't think I'll ever stop loving you. Not even if I tried. These past few days of waiting for you. Of wondering if you were ever going to . . . . And if you did—for how long? How would I ever keep you?"

"You don't have to keep me, because I'm not going anywhere. This is what I want. *You* are the only man I want to be with."

"But for how long?"

"You fell in love with me in ten minutes," she said softly. "What's to stop you from falling out of love just as fast?"

"That's not who I am."

"What's your guarantee?"

"There's no such thing."

"For anyone, Ty. Not even me. All I can tell you is that there's a hole in my heart right now that only you can fill. You've made me feel things that I didn't think I was capable of feeling. You held a mirror for me, you made me see who I am, made me realize that I didn't have to define myself by success. I love you, Ty. I'm standing here, stripped down to my heart. And I give it to you. You don't have to keep it or worry that it will run away. It's already yours. *I* am already yours."

He crossed the room in three steps and pulled her into his arms. Kari gave a small cry of joy and wrapped herself around him. She took his face in her hands and kissed him with all the indescribable, terrifying, wonderful emotions inside her. While his Christmas tree twinkled in the corner and Buttercup wagged her tail and danced at their feet, Kari gave all of herself to this man who'd peeled back the layers and been tender with the vulnerable woman inside.

They'd started with sex, but today, while winter cloaked the small town of Starlight Bend and froze the stars in the sky, they made love. The kind that bound a man and woman together for all of forever. The kind that unified and defined. There were no chains needed in this love. No locks that couldn't be broken. There was only the promise of tomorrow.

As they came together, Kari whispered, "I love you, Ty Timberlake."

He lifted his head and stared into her eyes. Gentle hands smoothed back her hair. He kissed the tip of her nose. "I love you, too, Kari with a K. You're what I wished for this Christmas."

She beamed at him. "My wish was granted, too. This is what I've always wanted, it just took me awhile to figure it out."

And with that heartbreaker smile she'd fallen in love with from the start, Ty lifted her off her feet and kissed her again. Kari kissed him back, letting him know that his long, gone girl had come home to stay.

CHAPTER TWENTY-THREE

THE STORM KEPT them housebound for all of the next day. Kari was glad for it. She and Ty spent it in bed, being in love. It was the greatest Christmas gift ever. They talked between kisses, laughed between warm caresses, and made love between meals. Each moment was one to be treasured and Kari soaked it in, lapped it up. This was the first day of forever and she wouldn't have changed a moment of it.

She called Simone later that morning and told her that after the deal was finalized, she planned to move on—or rather stay. Here. Simone wasn't the least bit surprised.

"You know, I wish you only the best, right? I think you're crazy, but Ty seems like a good guy."

"He is. He makes me happy."

Well, enough said, then."

"Actually, there's one more thing. I'd like to buy the hardware store."

"Sure. You want all of them?"

"No. Just the one in Starlight Bend."

"Really? What in the world are you going to do with it?"

"Great things, Simone. Great things."

Simone laughed. "Be sure to let me know if your stock goes public."

Christmas Eve dawned bright and crisp the next day, filled with a glimmer of sunshine that hinted at a clearing of the storm. Ty called around and by that afternoon, the doorbell began to ring. Friends in snowshoes and parkas came by with food and drink and laughter.

Kari recognized so many of them and felt warmed by their smiles and their greetings. They were willing to accept her. All she'd ever needed to do was open herself up. Even Marianne gave her a hug. "Good for you. He's worth fighting for," she whispered in Kari's ear. At her side was her fiancé, who was also one of the young fireman who'd responded to the fire alarm. Stan was there, too.

"I was talking to my Chief about that little gadget you have. He wants to see it," he said.

"Funny you should mention that. It just so happens, I own a hardware store and I have a storage locker back home that's filled with little gadgets I'm going to find a way to share. The Pocket Alarm will be the first on the list."

Ty's father was the last to arrive. On his arm was Becky Smith, who looked beautifully bright-eyed and rosy-cheeked. Henry smiled and blushed every time he glanced her way.

"Looking mighty fine in those jeans, Henry," Kari teased. And because it was Christmas she gave him a big hug. "Good catch," she whispered in his ear.

Becky laughed. "Yeah, he chased me so hard I finally caught him."

"I know exactly what you mean," Ty said, grinning at Kari.

Her heart was full and her life suddenly stretched out like a summer day, filled with sunshine, love and friends. Not a train track was in sight, and yet she still had plans. Still had goals. They simply complimented the scenery now, instead of cutting through it and marring everything they left behind. Never again would she be the long gone girl, laying tracks and moving on. She was here to stay.

Humming along with *Have Yourself a Merry Little Christmas* Kari decided she would have herself a Merry Little Life as well. Right here, in Starlight Bend with the most amazing man in the entire world.

EPILOGUE

SARA, AGE FOURTEEN—average size, average weight, average everything—didn't believe in Santa Claus. She didn't believe in much of anything, anymore. Christmas had no magic and tomorrow, a doubtful outcome. But her little brother and sister still believed and that was important. In a few weeks, their mom would be out of rehab for the second time, and their lives would either take a turn for the better or a hard left for a chaotic worse. Again.

She couldn't think of that now, though. All she could do was put on a happy face for her siblings and try not to worry herself into an early grave.

The Santa delivering gifts this year looked very real. His white hair and beard had a natural fluff and sheen. No elastic bands holding them in place. When he bent over, his hat even fell off—and the hair stayed in place—except for the shiny bald spot in the back. Ha. As close to a Christmas miracle as Sara ever hoped to see.

He knew their names, too. That alone was startling. One year, the Santa had called her, "Eleven-year-old girl." Yeah. That had been a Christmas moment to remember. At least he hadn't called her an eleven-year-old indigent.

Max got his gift first and waited patiently for Alyssa to take hers, thank Santa, and sit down. They'd been taught to wait before opening them—just in case the kind giver had bought them the same thing, regardless of the fact that they had different genders and ages. It happened, they all knew. But this Santa *ho-ho-ho'ed* and told them to go ahead.

When Max yanked the enormous *Wookie* out of the wrapping paper, Sara smiled for reals. Fingers crossed, she watched Alyssa go to town on her wrapped package and lo-and-behold . . . out came the deluxe version of a *Loopdedoo Kit.*

Sara almost cried at the excitement on their faces. She said a silent thank you to the powers that be and knelt down to admire their gifts. She didn't hear Santa call her name until Max nudged her.

"Sara, he's got one for you."

Surprised, Sara looked up as Santa handed her a big package. Big and square, shifty in the middle, like maybe there were two boxes stacked together and held by the wrapping paper and ribbon.

Too surprised to say anything but a mumbled, "Thanks," Sara took the package and opened it.

She'd been right: two boxes. Someone had written on the lids of each one in sparkly red and green marker. "What you asked for" on the first, and "What you really want," on the second.

She hadn't asked for anything, though.

Intrigued, Sara opened the first one first—what she'd asked for. Inside, she found jeans, a top, even new underclothes, all from Abercrombie kids—a store she'd only heard about. She'd never be able to afford it, so she'd never tried to go to one. But of course other kids at school wore their clothes. Cool kids, which Sara was not.

Her fingers trailed over the fabric as she pictured herself wearing the outfit to school. Kids who always whispered about her second-hand clothes would have to shut up for once.

"Just clothes," Max said, looking over her shoulder with disappointment as he waved his Wookie around.

"But pretty," Alyssa said, though she was obviously equally unimpressed by the brand name attire some stranger had picked out just for Sara.

Nervous excitement bunched up in her stomach as she reached for the second box. *What You Want.*

Tissue paper with stars and unicorns hid the contents inside the box. On top, attached by a bright green seal, was a card with her name on it.

Dear Sara, it read. *This was made by a high school student not much older than you. I found it on Etsy and I just knew you'd love it. I hope I'm right. Your note on the Wish Tree touched me, Sara, and I'd like to help you and your family. When your mom gets on her feet again, tell her to call me at the number below. I have a job offer for her.*

A job? Seriously? Her mother had a record now and Sara had spent many sleepless nights wondering how they would live, eat. You know, little things like that.

In a daze, she read the last lines of the card. *Merry Christmas. Never stop believing. Kari.*

Never stop? Sara had never had the chance to *start* believing. But as she pulled out the long dress with its wild pattern and intricate lace work, she felt a little of that Christmas magic swirling inside her. The dress was beautiful, funky, so unique and colorful that it shouted, *look at me. I don't care what you think.* It was perfect in every way. The box held shoes, too. Low boots with an elfin cuff in a pearly peach color.

She held the dress up to her and knew it would fit like a dream.

Santa was watching her with a smile on his face. "Hold your head high, Sara. Life has big plans for you."

And with a booming, *Ho Ho Ho,* Santa left to make his next stop. As Sara, Max, and Alyssa stared at one another with wide eyes and opened mouths, they heard sleigh bells ringing and Santa's jolly, "Merry Christmas," echoing behind him.

And for the first time in her very young life, Sara, age fourteen, felt better than average. In fact, she felt like maybe, just maybe, this Merry Christmas might lead to a very Happy New Year.

DEAR READER,

Thank you for reading *The Long Gone Girl of Starlight Bend.* I hope you enjoyed Kari and Ty's story as much as I enjoyed writing it. If you liked this tale, you might want to check out Kissing Kris Kringle, another Christmas story set in the small town of North Pole, Maine.

For more information about that book and all of my others which include Time Travel set in Ireland, dark paranormal, set in Arizona (think Supernatural meets Joe Black), and historical set in the United States, please visit www.ErinQuinnBooks.com where you can sign up for my newsletter and contests!

You can also follow me on Facebook, Twitter or Instagram @ErinQuinnAuthor.

Whatever your beliefs and traditions, I wish you the happiest of holidays and the best New Year ever!

Erin Quinn

PS: If you're a whiskey drinker and wondering at my use of "whiskey" instead of "whisky," rest assured I did my homework and chose whiskey with an "e" because Kari and Ty are drinking Jameson Irish Whiskey, which is spelled with an "e." Had they instead been drinking Scotch whisky, Glenfiddich malt whisky for example, the "e" would have been banished. #nowyouknow

About the Author

New York Times and USA Today Bestselling author Erin Quinn writes dark paranormal romance for the thinking reader and light romantic comedy for the reader who just wants to have fun. Her books have been called "riveting," "brilliantly plotted" and "beautifully written" and have won, placed or showed in numerous awards including the prestigious RWA RITA award. Go to **www.erinquinnbooks.com**. Look for the third book in the Beyond Series, The Seven Sins of Ruby Love in 2017. The Mists of Ireland will be re-released in digital and print early 2017.

BOOKS BY ERIN QUINN

THE BEYOND SERIES

THE FIVE DEATHS OF ROXANNE LOVE (BOOK 1)

THE FORBIDDEN LIFE OF ALEX MOORE (NOVELLA 1.5)
RITA Finalist

THE THREE FATES OF RYAN LOVE (BOOK 2)

THE RESURRECTION OF SAM SLOAN (NOVELLA 2.5)

THE SEVEN SINS OF RUBY LOVE (BOOK 3)
Coming April 2017

THE MISTS OF IRELAND SERIES (TIME TRAVEL)

HAUNTING BEAUTY (BOOK 1)

HAUNTING WARRIOR (BOOK 2)

HAUNTING DESIRE (BOOK 3)

HAUNTING EMBRACE (BOOK 4)

STAND ALONE TITLES

DIABLO SPRINGS
Paranormal Romance

ECHOES (COMING SOON)
Paranormal Romance

HOLIDAY STORIES

KISSING KRIS KRINGLE
Part of the *Sexy Secret Santa Collection*

SHAKING IT UP
Part of the *With a Twist Valentine's Collection*

A LITTLE BIT OF SUGAR
Part of the *Snowed In and Snuggled Up Thanksgiving Collection*

For a complete book list of Erin Quinn's titles, go to
http://www.erinquinnbooks.com